More Ghost Stories of
an Antiquary

*More Timeless Gothic Horror Tales – Haunting
Encounters from a Legendary Ghost Storyteller*

A Modern Translation

Adapted for the Contemporary Reader

M.R. James

Translated by Tim Zengerink

Table of Contents

Preface - Message to the Reader

What If You Could Help Rebuild the Greatest Library in Human History?

Thousands of years ago, the Library of Alexandria stood as the crown jewel of human achievement — a sanctuary where the collected wisdom of every known civilization was gathered, preserved, and shared freely.

And then, it was lost.

Through fire, conquest, and the slow erosion of time, humanity lost not just books — but ideas, dreams, discoveries, and stories that could have changed the world forever.

Today, the Library of Alexandria lives again — and you are invited to be a part of its restoration.

Our mission is simple yet profound:

To rebuild the greatest library the world has ever known, and to translate all timeless works into every language and dialect, so that no seeker of knowledge is ever left behind again.

By joining our movement to rebuild the modern Library of Alexandria, you become part of an unprecedented mission:

- **Unlimited Access to the Greatest Audiobooks & eBooks Ever Written:**

  Instantly explore thousands of legendary works—Plato, Shakespeare, Jane Austen, Leo Tolstoy, and countless more. All instantly available to read or listen, placing a complete literary universe at your fingertips.

- **Beautiful Paperback & Deluxe Editions at Printing Cost**

  Own any title as an elegant paperback, deluxe hardcover, or stunning collectible boxset—offered to you at true printing cost, delivered straight to your door. Build your personal Library of Alexandria, crafted for beauty, built for durability, and worthy of proud display.

- **Fresh Translations for Modern Readers—in Every Language & Dialect**

  Enjoy timeless masterpieces reimagined in clear, contemporary language—no more outdated phrases or obscure references. Alongside the original versions, we're tirelessly translating these classics into every language and dialect imaginable, ensuring accessibility and understanding across cultures and generations.

- **Join a Global Renaissance of Literature & Knowledge**

  You directly support expanding our library, publishing deluxe editions at true cost, translating works into all global languages, and bringing humanity's greatest stories to people everywhere. By joining today, you're not just preserving a legacy of masterpieces; you set in motion a powerful wave of literary accessibility.

Become a Torchbearer of Knowledge.

Join us for free now at **LibraryofAlexandria.com**

Together, we will ensure that the light of human wisdom never fades again.

With gratitude and a shared love of knowledge,

The Modern Library of Alexandria Team

Visit:

www.libraryofalexandria.com

Or scan the code below:

Introduction

The Scholar of Shadows:
M.R. James's Evolving Craft of Supernatural Fiction

With the 1911 publication of More Ghost Stories of an Antiquary, M.R. James firmly established himself not only as the foremost ghost story writer of his generation but also as the creator of a wholly new form of supernatural fiction—one rooted in intellectualism, restraint, and suggestion rather than sensationalism. This second volume of ghostly tales, following the critical success of Ghost Stories of an Antiquary (1904), showcases James at the height of his imaginative and narrative powers. The stories in this collection—eight in total—further refine the Jamesian aesthetic, demonstrating an even greater command of atmosphere, pacing, and the calculated use of terror.

Where the first volume introduced readers to James's signature style—dry wit, antiquarian protagonists, and ghosts that haunt not through flamboyant menace but with cold precision—More Ghost Stories of an Antiquary deepens those themes. The tales here are more structurally complex, more psychologically intimate, and more daring in their implications. They exhibit James's belief that a ghost story should be both entertaining and disturbing, offering what he once described as "a pleasing terror." The stories do not rely on shock; instead, they unnerve slowly, inexorably, with an eerie finality that lingers long after the last sentence.

From the malevolent vengeance of "The Tractate Middoth" to the surreal, ambiguous horror of "The Residence at Whitminster," James shows an impressive versatility in both narrative voice and thematic depth. He is no longer merely experimenting with the genre—he is shaping it. In these pages, readers will find further proof of James's commitment to a ghost story tradition rooted in scholarly realism and historical detail, paired with just enough suggestion of the supernatural to set the imagination ablaze. The result is a series of stories that resist over-explanation and remain potent in their ambiguity.

James's use of framing devices, marginalia, and textual artifacts continues here, as does his signature technique of grounding the supernatural within the familiar. His ghosts remain profoundly physical—capable of leaving hair, footprints, fingermarks, or simply a cold presence—but never fully explained. These are not spirits with backstories and resolutions, but embodiments of cosmic or moral forces, called forth by curiosity, violation, or accident. The lessons are rarely moral in a traditional sense. The punishment often fits no crime. And that unpredictability is part of what makes these tales so unnerving.

Between Antiquity and Dread:
Stories of Knowledge, Objects, and Place

Like the first volume, More Ghost Stories of an Antiquary centers on men of learning—clergymen, librarians, scholars, and collectors—who unwittingly disturb the veil between the seen and the unseen. James, himself a Cambridge academic and medievalist, injects each story with the air of the archival, the ecclesiastical, the carefully catalogued. Yet he never allows erudition to smother suspense. Instead, he shows how deeply intellectual inquiry can lead one astray when it encounters the limits of human understanding.

In "The Tractate Middoth," for instance, a simple search for a rare book becomes a brush with a ghostly curse tied to inheritance, family secrets, and death. In "Casting the Runes," arguably one of James's most beloved stories, the protagonist is targeted by an occult scholar whose written papers are vehicles for death—a terrifying metaphor for the unseen power of knowledge and words. Here, the ghost story morphs into something close to a psychological thriller, with chase scenes, coded warnings, and an adversary as cunning as he is sinister.

What makes these stories resonate is the precision of James's world-building. His locations are not dreamlike or amorphous, but clearly mapped: libraries, seaside inns, lecture halls, dusty studies, cathedral towns. These settings ground the reader in the known and the ordinary, which makes the intrusion of the supernatural all the more jarring. James's ghosts are not intruding into fairy tales—they are stepping into the waking world, into polite English society, and into the minds of unsuspecting men who, until that moment, believed themselves to be entirely safe.

In "The Rose Garden," a seemingly peaceful estate reveals its dark past through a haunting tied to repressed history and forgotten violence. And in "Martin's Close," James employs a courtroom drama framework to unravel a ghostly retribution tale, using the cold language of legal testimony to build suspense and deliver uncanny revelations. The brilliance of these tales lies not in elaborate plot twists, but in James's ability to render the familiar strange, to peel back the respectable surface of daily life and reveal the dark folklore and buried sins beneath.

James's characters are rarely evil. They are curious, and sometimes careless. What they suffer is rarely unjust—but it is always unexplained. They are punished not because they have sinned, but because they have wandered too close to the edges of human knowledge, to those forbidden corners of history where ancient pacts, monstrous entities, and supernatural forces still linger.

This sense of lurking dread—this idea that reality is thinner than we think, and that something terrible watches from the other side—defines the Jamesian ghost story. It is not a genre of catharsis, but of unease. The reader is not granted closure, only a glimpse into the unknown, and then the curtain is drawn once again.

Literary Impact, Cultural Legacy, and the Modern Reader

By the time More Ghost Stories of an Antiquary was published, M.R. James had already begun to influence a generation of writers, both within Britain and abroad. His ghost stories were read aloud at Christmas gatherings, adapted for radio, television, and film, and imitated by a legion of authors from the mid-20th century to the present day. His style—formal, detailed, and tinged with humor—became a benchmark of supernatural restraint, a sharp contrast to the lurid horror and gothic excess that had previously dominated the genre.

Writers such as H.P. Lovecraft, Robert Aickman, Susan Hill, and Ramsey Campbell have all acknowledged their debt to James. Lovecraft, in particular, admired James's technique of suggestion—of never fully describing the ghost or explaining its origins. James understood, perhaps better than anyone before him, that what is left unsaid can be more terrifying than what is shown. His ghosts do not rant or perform. They creep, they whisper, they linger at the edge of sleep or sanity. They do not need to justify themselves. They simply are.

James also helped solidify the idea that ghost stories could be both literary and chilling. He never sacrificed narrative elegance for easy scares. His stories are structured with meticulous care—rising tension, subtle foreshadowing, climactic terror, and abrupt, unsettling resolution. He rarely moralizes. Instead, he leaves readers with questions—about knowledge, history, and the limits of perception.

This modern edition of More Ghost Stories of an Antiquary seeks to honor James's style and spirit while rendering his prose more accessible to contemporary readers. While his stories remain masterpieces of early 20th-century literature, their language—dense with Victorian syntax, Latin phrases, and ecclesiastical formality—can be a barrier to modern audiences. In this edition, archaic phrasing and overly complex constructions have been subtly modernized for clarity and flow, without altering the tone or narrative rhythm. The ghosts remain. The dread remains. But the pathway to them has been made smoother.

Reading this collection today, over a century after its publication, is a reminder of how potent subtle horror can be. James's stories do not rely on violence, gore, or graphic horror. They rely on suggestion, atmosphere, and the slow dawning of a terrible realization. They show that the supernatural is not necessarily loud or theatrical—it is patient, meticulous, and profoundly quiet.

This edition invites you to read as James intended—perhaps in the evening, with a dim light, when the house is silent. These are stories not meant to startle, but to echo. To leave a trace. To settle like dust on the skin and memory. In them, you will find ancient whispers, buried warnings, and shadows that do not move when they should. And perhaps, if you read closely enough, you too will hear the voice at the edge of the silence—the ghost of the antiquary himself, still telling tales.

Canon Alberic's Scrap-Book

St. Bertrand de Comminges is a small, old town at the edge of the Pyrenees, not far from Toulouse and even closer to Bagnères-de-Luchon. It used to have a bishop until the French Revolution, and it still has a cathedral that attracts some tourists. In the spring of 1883, an Englishman came to visit this quiet place. It's too small to call a city—it has fewer than a thousand people.

This Englishman, who had studied at Cambridge, had traveled from Toulouse just to see the church at St. Bertrand. He left two friends behind at their hotel in Toulouse because they weren't as interested in old buildings. They agreed to meet him the next morning. His friends figured half an hour at the church would be enough, and after that, the three of them planned to continue on to Auch.

But this man came early, determined to spend the whole day taking notes and photographs of every part of the church, which sits high on a hill above the town. To do this properly, he needed the help of the church's caretaker, known as the verger or sacristan (even if that's not the exact title). The woman who ran the local inn, the Chapeau Rouge, sent for the sacristan on his behalf.

When the sacristan arrived, the Englishman found him more interesting than he expected—not because of how he looked (he resembled many old church caretakers in France), but because of the strange way he acted. The little man seemed nervous and jittery, always glancing over his shoulder like someone was chasing him. His shoulders were tight and hunched, as if he was always bracing for something bad to happen. Dennistoun, as we'll call the Englishman, wasn't sure what to make of him. Was the man paranoid? Hiding something? Or maybe just scared of his wife? That last guess seemed most likely, but there was still something more serious and unsettling about his behavior.

Soon, though, Dennistoun got caught up in his work. He was focused on filling his notebook and snapping pictures, only looking at the sacristan every now and then. But each time he did, the old man was never far off—either pressed up against the wall or crouching in one of the decorative wooden choir seats.

After a while, Dennistoun started to feel a little awkward. He wondered if the old man was missing lunch, or if maybe he thought Dennistoun was going to steal something valuable—like the old ivory staff of St. Bertrand or the dusty stuffed crocodile that hung above the baptismal font.

"Why don't you head home?" Dennistoun finally asked. "I'm fine on my own. You can lock the door if you're worried. I'll be here for at least two more hours. Aren't you cold?"

The old man looked absolutely horrified at the suggestion. "No, no, monsieur must not be left alone in the church! Not for a moment. I've already had my breakfast, and I'm not cold at all—thank you."

"All right," Dennistoun thought to himself. "You've been warned. Whatever happens now is on you."

By the time the two hours were up, Dennistoun had carefully studied everything—the choir stalls, the huge broken organ, the carved screen made by Bishop John de Mauléon, the old stained glass, the faded tapestries, and the items in the treasure room. The sacristan never left his side. He kept jumping and turning around whenever one of the strange sounds of the big empty church echoed through the halls.

Dennistoun later told me, "Once, I could've sworn I heard a high-pitched metallic laugh coming from the tower. I looked at the sacristan. His face was pale as chalk. He just said, 'It's him—or I mean—it's no one. The door is locked.' And then we stared at each other for a full minute."

Another moment left Dennistoun confused. He was studying a large, dark painting that hangs behind the altar. It's one of several showing the miracles of St. Bertrand. The image was almost too faded to make out, but underneath it, in Latin, was a caption that read:

How St. Bertrand Saved a Man the Devil Tried to Strangle for a Long Time.

Dennistoun was about to make a joke to the sacristan when he noticed something strange. The old man had dropped to his knees and was staring at the painting with a look of deep pain, as if he were begging for help. His hands were clenched together, and tears were running down his face. Dennistoun acted like he hadn't seen it, but the moment stayed with him. Why would such a faded old painting affect someone so strongly? He began to wonder if the man was obsessed with something. But what exactly was his obsession?

It was almost five o'clock now. The short winter day was coming to an end, and shadows began to fill the church. The strange noises—soft footsteps and distant whispers—that had been there all day seemed to grow louder and more frequent as the light faded.

For the first time, the sacristan began to show signs of impatience. He seemed relieved when Dennistoun finally packed up his notebook and camera. The old man quickly motioned for him to head toward the western door of the church, the one beneath the tower. It was time to ring the Angelus—a traditional prayer call. He gave a few strong pulls on the heavy bell rope, and high above them, the big bell, named

Bertrande, began to ring. Its sound echoed across the pine-covered hills and down into the valleys, where mountain streams ran. It called out for people to remember the angel's message to Mary, the one called "blessed among women."

With that, a deep silence settled over the little town—maybe for the first time that day—and the two men stepped out of the church.

As they stood on the steps, they started to talk.

"You seemed interested in the old choir books in the sacristy," the sacristan said.

"Yes," said Dennistoun. "Actually, I was going to ask if there's a library in town."

"No, monsieur," the sacristan replied. "There may have been one in the past, for the church chapter, but the town is very small now—" He paused suddenly, as if unsure whether to say more. Then, as if making up his mind, he continued, "But if monsieur is a lover of old books, I have something at home you might want to see. It's only a short walk."

Dennistoun's imagination lit up. He dreamed of finding rare, forgotten books in out-of-the-way places in France. But then he quickly calmed down—it was probably just an old prayer book printed by Plantin around 1580. Surely collectors had already searched towns this close to Toulouse. Still, it would be foolish to turn down the offer. He'd regret it forever if he said no.

As they walked, Dennistoun thought about the old man's strange hesitation and sudden decision. He started to feel a little nervous—was he being tricked? Would he be robbed or worse, as a foreigner who might seem rich? Just to be safe, he mentioned (awkwardly) that two of his friends would be joining him the next morning. To his surprise, the sacristan looked instantly relieved.

"That is good," he said, looking more cheerful. "Very good. It is always best to travel with friends… sometimes."

That last word—"sometimes"—sounded like an afterthought, and the man's gloom seemed to return.

Soon they reached the sacristan's home. It was a little larger than the other houses nearby, built of stone, with a carved family crest above the door—the crest of Alberic de Mauléon, a distant relative of Bishop John de Mauléon. Dennistoun learned that Alberic had been a church leader in Comminges from 1680 to 1701. The upper windows were boarded up, and the whole house looked old and worn down, just like the rest of the town.

At the doorstep, the sacristan hesitated.

"Perhaps," he said, "you don't really have the time after all?"

"No, not at all," Dennistoun replied. "I've got plenty of time and nothing planned until tomorrow. Let's see what you've got."

Just then, the door opened and a young woman peeked out. She was much younger than the sacristan, but her face showed the same troubled expression—though hers seemed more like worry for someone else than fear for herself. It was clear she was his daughter. If it weren't for the anxiety written on her face, she would have been quite pretty.

She seemed relieved to see her father with a healthy-looking visitor. The two spoke quietly for a moment, and Dennistoun only caught a few words. The sacristan said, "He was laughing in the church," and the girl responded with a terrified look.

Within minutes, they were inside the sitting room of the house. It was a small, high-ceilinged room with a cold stone floor. Shadows danced along the walls, cast by a flickering wood fire burning in a large fireplace. The space felt a bit like a small chapel, thanks to a tall crucifix that almost touched the ceiling on one side. The figure of Jesus was painted in lifelike colors, and the cross itself was black. Beneath it stood an old wooden chest.

After a lamp was brought in and chairs were placed, the sacristan went to the chest and, with what Dennistoun thought was growing excitement—or maybe nervousness—he pulled out a large book wrapped in a white cloth. There was a red cross stitched into the cloth, roughly done. Even before the cloth came off, Dennistoun felt his curiosity spark. The book was big—too large for a missal, and the wrong shape for an antiphoner. "Maybe this really is something special," he thought.

The book was opened, and in that moment, Dennistoun knew he'd found something far better than he'd imagined. In front of him was a large folio, probably bound in the late 1600s, with a golden crest stamped on the cover—Canon Alberic de Mauléon's. Inside were about 150 pages, each holding a leaf from a beautifully illustrated manuscript.

This was beyond anything Dennistoun had hoped to find. There were ten pages from an ancient copy of Genesis, likely from the year 700, each with colorful illustrations. Then came a complete set of pictures from a Psalter, done in England, showing the highest level of artistry from the 1200s. But maybe the most exciting discovery was a group of 20 pages written in old Latin, in large rounded letters. Even at a glance, Dennistoun realized these pages came from a very early and unknown religious text. Could it possibly be part of the lost work

On the Words of Our Lord by Papias, known to have existed in Nîmes during the 1100s? Whether it was or not, one thing was certain: he had to bring this book back to Cambridge—even if it meant emptying his bank account and staying in St. Bertrand until the money arrived.

He looked up at the sacristan to see if he might be willing to sell it. The old man looked pale, and his mouth twitched nervously.

"If monsieur will turn to the end," he said.

Dennistoun did so, finding more incredible pages with each turn. Then, at the very end, he came across two sheets of paper much newer than the rest of the book. He guessed they were from the same time as Canon Alberic, who had most likely stolen these manuscript pages from the church library to make this valuable scrapbook.

The first sheet showed a carefully drawn map of the south aisle and cloisters of St. Bertrand's. Dennistoun immediately recognized the layout. There were strange symbols on the page—some looked like astrology signs, and some Hebrew words were written in the corners. A gold-painted cross was marked in the northwest corner of the cloister. Below the drawing was a short message in Latin:

Answers from December 12, 1694.

Q: Will I find it?

A: You will.

Q: Will I become rich?

A: You will.

Q: Will I live an enviable life?

A: You will.

Q: Will I die in my own bed?

A: You will.

"A perfect example of a treasure-hunter's journal," Dennistoun muttered to himself. "Sounds like something out of Old St. Paul's." Then he turned the page.

What he saw next left a deeper impression on him than any artwork ever had—and he later said nothing else had ever shaken him the same way. The original drawing no longer exists, but a photograph of it survives (which the narrator owns), and it confirms everything Dennistoun felt.

The picture was done in brown ink around the end of the 1600s and looked like it was meant to show a Bible story. The setting was an indoor space with classical-style architecture. On the right side was a king sitting on a high throne, raised on twelve steps and covered with a canopy. Soldiers stood on either side of him. The king—clearly Solomon—was leaning forward with a scepter in his hand, giving a command. His face showed a mix of horror and disgust, but also strength and authority.

But it was the left side of the picture that drew all the attention.

In front of the throne, four soldiers stood around a crouching figure. One soldier lay dead nearby, his neck twisted, eyes bulging out. The others stared at the king with frightened faces. Their horror was clear—they were only staying because they trusted the king's power.

Whatever was crouched in the center had filled them with fear.

Words can't fully explain what that creature looked like. The narrator once showed the photo to a biology professor, a very logical man, who refused to be alone afterward. He later admitted that for several nights he was too afraid to turn off the lights before going to sleep.

The creature was covered in thick, tangled black hair. Beneath it, the body was sickeningly thin, like a skeleton with tight muscles stretched over it. Its skin was dull and gray, its hands clawed and hairy. Its eyes burned yellow, with jet-black pupils, and it stared at the king with pure animal hatred. Imagine one of those terrifying, spider-like creatures from South America turned into something almost human—intelligent, but just barely—and you'll begin to understand the horror this figure created.

Everyone who sees the image says the same thing:

"This had to be drawn from real life."

As soon as Dennistoun calmed down a little, he looked at the father and daughter. The sacristan had his hands over his eyes, and his daughter was staring up at the cross on the wall, whispering prayers quickly and nervously.

Finally, Dennistoun asked, "Is the book for sale?"

There was a short pause—just like before—then the sacristan gave the answer he'd been hoping for: "If you wish, monsieur."

"How much are you asking for it?"

"I'll take two hundred and fifty francs."

Dennistoun was surprised. Even collectors sometimes feel guilty, and he was more thoughtful than most.

"My good man," he said, "this book is worth much more than that. A lot more, I promise you."

But the sacristan didn't change his mind. "Two hundred and fifty francs. No more."

Dennistoun couldn't pass up the offer. He paid the money, signed a receipt, and they shared a glass of wine to seal the deal. After that, the old man seemed like a different person—he stood straighter, stopped glancing nervously around, and even managed a laugh.

Dennistoun got up to leave.

"I'll walk you back to your hotel," the sacristan offered.

"No, thank you," Dennistoun said. "It's not far, I know the way, and the moon's out."

The sacristan offered again and again, but Dennistoun kindly turned him down each time.

"Well then, if monsieur needs anything, he will send for me, yes? And please, walk in the middle of the road. The sides are rough."

"Of course," said Dennistoun, eager to be alone with the book. He stepped into the hallway, carrying it under his arm.

The sacristan's daughter was waiting there. She seemed to have her own plan in mind—maybe hoping to get a little something from the visitor her father had just helped.

She held out a silver cross on a chain. "Would monsieur accept this?" she asked kindly.

Dennistoun didn't really know what to say. "How much do you want for it?"

"Nothing at all," she said. "It's a gift. You're more than welcome to have it."

Her tone made it clear she truly meant it. Dennistoun thanked her many times and let her put the chain around his neck. It felt like he'd helped them in some way, though he couldn't imagine how.

As he walked back to his hotel, he saw them standing in the doorway, still watching him. They were looking on as he gave them one last wave from the steps of the Chapeau Rouge.

After dinner, Dennistoun was finally alone in his room with the book. The landlady had shown extra interest after he mentioned buying it from the sacristan. He thought he heard her speaking quietly with the old man in the hallway. The last thing he caught was, "Pierre and Bertrand will be sleeping in the house tonight."

By then, an odd feeling had started to creep over him. Maybe it was just nerves from the excitement of the day, but he kept getting the sense someone was behind him. It felt better to sit with his back against the wall.

Still, he told himself it didn't matter compared to the amazing value of the book. Every page he turned revealed something new and fascinating. He couldn't believe his luck.

"Bless Canon Alberic," he said out loud—he often talked to himself. "I wonder what happened to him. Honestly, I wish the landlady wouldn't laugh like that. It sounds like someone died here. Another puff of the pipe? Yeah, probably a good idea."

He picked up the crucifix the young woman had given him. "I wonder what this is exactly. Looks like it was made sometime last century. Kind of heavy to wear. Her father probably wore it for years. I should clean it before I put it away."

He had just taken off the crucifix and set it on the table when he noticed something lying on the red cloth near his left elbow. His mind raced with guesses.

"A penwiper? No, nothing like that here. A rat? No, too dark. A spider? I hope not—wait... oh no. It's a hand. A hand like the one in that drawing!"

In an instant, he saw it clearly. The skin was pale and grayish, stretched tightly over thin bones and powerful tendons. Thick black hairs stuck out from it—too long to be human. The fingers ended in long, curved nails, gray and rough like old claws.

Dennistoun jumped back from the chair, frozen with fear. The thing that had rested its left hand on the table was now rising to stand right behind him. Its right hand was lifted above his head. It wore black, ragged clothes, and its body was covered in that same coarse hair—just like in the picture. Its lower jaw was thin and animal-like, with sharp teeth behind cracked black lips. It had no nose. Its yellow eyes, with dark black pupils, glared with a terrifying, almost human hatred and a wild hunger to destroy. The eyes were the worst part. There was a cruel intelligence in them—smarter than a beast but not fully human.

Dennistoun felt absolute terror and deep disgust. He didn't know what to do. He's never been sure what he said out loud, but he remembers reaching blindly for the silver crucifix, sensing the monster move toward him, and then letting out a scream—raw and full of pain, like an animal.

Pierre and Bertrand, the two small but tough house servants, ran in. They didn't see anything, but both were shoved aside by something rushing past them. They found Dennistoun passed out on the floor.

They stayed with him all night. By nine the next morning, his two friends had arrived in St. Bertrand. Though still shaken, Dennistoun had mostly recovered, and after showing them the drawing and talking with the sacristan, they believed his story.

Just before dawn, the old sacristan came to the inn with some excuse. He listened closely to the landlady's retelling of the story, but didn't seem surprised.

"It was him. I've seen him with my own eyes," he said quietly.

That was all he would say. Whenever they asked more, his only answer was, "I've seen him twice; I've felt his presence a thousand times." He never explained where the book came from or what exactly he had been through.

"I'll be sleeping soon," he said. "And it will be a peaceful rest. Why trouble me now?"

He died that summer. His daughter later got married and moved to St. Papoul. She never really understood what had haunted her father.

We'll never truly know what the sacristan or Canon Alberic de Mauléon experienced. But on the back of that terrifying drawing, some writing was found that might give us a clue:

The Dispute of Solomon with a night demon. Drawn by Alberic de Mauléon.

Verse: O Lord, come quickly to help me.

Psalm: He who dwells in the secret place... (Psalm 91).

Saint Bertrand, chaser of demons, pray for me, a miserable man.

I saw it first on the night of December 12, 1694. I will see it for the last time soon.

I have sinned and suffered—and I will suffer more. December 29, 1701.

According to church records, Canon Alberic died suddenly in bed on December 31, 1701. It's rare for those records to include details like that.

Dennistoun never fully explained what he believed about what happened. Once, he quoted from the book of Ecclesiasticus: "Some spirits are created for vengeance, and in their fury bring harsh punishment." Another time he said, "Isaiah had it right, didn't he? Didn't he say something about night creatures living in the ruins of Babylon? Maybe these things are just beyond our understanding."

There was one thing he said that really stayed with me. Last year, we visited Comminges to see Canon Alberic's grave. It's a huge marble tomb with a statue of the canon in a big wig and priest's robes, with a long message about how wise and learned he was. Dennistoun spent a while speaking with the local priest. As we drove away, he said to me, "I hope it's not wrong to say this—you know I'm a Presbyterian—but I think there'll be prayers and songs for Canon Alberic's soul."

Then, with a wry smile, he added, "I didn't know they charged so much for that kind of thing."

The book now belongs to the Wentworth Collection in Cambridge. As for the drawing—it was photographed, then burned by Dennistoun the same day he left Comminges after that first visit.

Lost Hearts

It was sometime in September of 1811 when a carriage stopped in front of Aswarby Hall, deep in the countryside of Lincolnshire. A young boy, the only passenger, quickly jumped out and looked around with excitement while he waited for someone to answer the door.

He saw a tall, square-shaped house made of red brick. It had been built during Queen Anne's time, with a stone porch added later in a more classical style from the 1790s. The windows were tall and narrow, with small panes and thick white frames. A triangular roof piece with a round window sat above the front door.

On both sides of the house were wings connected to the main building by glass-covered walkways held up by columns. These side sections clearly held the stables and servants' areas, and each one had a fancy little tower with a golden weather vane on top.

The evening sun lit the building, making the windows glow as if fires were burning inside. In front of the house stretched a flat park dotted with oak trees and edged with fir trees. A church tower peeked out from the trees at the edge of the property, and its golden weathercock gleamed in the light. As the clock struck six, its soft chimes floated across the air.

It all made a peaceful, almost dreamlike scene—calm but touched by the quiet sadness that often comes with autumn evenings. That was how it felt to the boy as he waited at the door.

The carriage had brought him all the way from Warwickshire. Six months earlier, he'd lost both his parents. Now, thanks to an offer from his older cousin Mr. Abney, he was coming to live at Aswarby Hall.

The offer had come as a surprise. Everyone who knew Mr. Abney thought of him as a quiet, serious man who mostly kept to himself. It was strange to imagine a boy living in such a quiet, grown-up household.

Not much was really known about Mr. Abney's daily life or personality. A professor at Cambridge had once said that no one knew more about the old religions of ancient times than Mr. Abney. His library was full of rare books on ancient mystery cults, the Orphic poems, the worship of Mithras, and writings by the Neo-Platonists.

In the marble-floored entrance hall, there was a statue of the god Mithras killing a bull—a rare piece that Mr. Abney had imported from the Middle East at great cost. He had written about it for The Gentleman's Magazine and had published articles in The Critical Museum about the superstitions of the later Roman Empire.

People saw him as someone completely absorbed in books, so it was a shock to the locals when he not only remembered his orphaned cousin, Stephen Elliott, but also offered to take him in.

Despite the rumors, Mr. Abney—tall, thin, and serious—seemed genuinely happy to welcome Stephen. As soon as the front door opened, he rushed out of his study, rubbing his hands together with excitement.

"How are you, my boy? How old are you?" he said. "You're not too tired to eat, I hope?"

"No, thank you, sir," Stephen replied politely. "I feel fine."

"Good, good!" said Mr. Abney. "And how old are you?"

It was a little odd that he asked the same question again so soon.

"I'll be twelve on my next birthday, sir."

"And when is that? September eleventh, is it? Excellent—very good! That's nearly a year from now, isn't it? I like to write these things down in my notebook. You're sure it's twelve?"

"Yes, I'm sure."

"Very well then. Parkes, take him to Mrs. Bunch's room for tea— or supper, whichever it is."

"Yes, sir," replied the butler, Mr. Parkes, and he led Stephen downstairs.

Mrs. Bunch, the housekeeper, was the warmest and most welcoming person Stephen had met so far. Within fifteen minutes, they were fast friends—and they stayed that way.

She had been born nearby more than fifty-five years earlier and had worked at the Hall for the last twenty years. If anyone knew all the secrets of the house and garden, it was her. She was also happy to share what she knew.

There were plenty of things Stephen wanted to ask about. He was naturally curious and loved exploring. "Who built that temple at the end of the laurel path? Who's the old man in the painting on the stairs—the one with his hand on a skull?"

Mrs. Bunch had answers to most of his questions. But there were a few things she couldn't—or wouldn't—explain clearly.

One evening in November, Stephen was sitting by the fire in Mrs. Bunch's cozy room, thinking about everything.

"Is Mr. Abney a good man? Will he go to heaven?" he asked suddenly. Like many children, he believed grown-ups could answer deep questions easily.

"Good? Bless the child!" said Mrs. Bunch. "Master's as kind a soul as ever I saw! Didn't I ever tell you about the little boy he took in off the street about seven years ago? And the little girl he brought here two years after I first came to work?"

"No, you never told me," said Stephen eagerly. "Please tell me now—right now!"

"Well," Mrs. Bunch said, "I don't remember the little girl all that well. I just know Master brought her home one day after one of his walks and told Mrs. Ellis, who worked here before me, to take good care of her. The poor child didn't have any family—she told me that herself. She stayed here for about three weeks. Then one morning, before anyone woke up, she disappeared. No one ever found out what happened. Master was heartbroken. He even had the ponds searched. I always thought the gypsies took her. People had been singing near the house the night before, and Parkes swore he heard voices in the woods that afternoon. She was a quiet little thing—but very sweet and polite. I really liked her."

"And what about the little boy?" Stephen asked.

"Oh, that poor boy," Mrs. Bunch sighed. "He was a foreigner—called himself Jevanny. He was playing his hurdy-gurdy near the driveway one winter day, and Master invited him inside right away. He asked him where he was from, how old he was, and if he had any family. He was very kind to him. But just like the girl, the boy vanished one morning. No one ever figured out why or where he went. He even left his hurdy-gurdy behind—it's still sitting on the shelf."

Stephen spent the rest of the evening asking Mrs. Bunch more questions and trying to make music with the hurdy-gurdy.

That night, he had a strange dream.

At the far end of the hallway near his room, there was an old bathroom no one used anymore. The door was always locked, but the top half had glass. Since the curtains had been missing for a long time, you could look through and see the old bathtub under the window.

In his dream, Stephen was standing in front of that door, peeking in. The moonlight came through the window, lighting up the tub. Inside was something eerie.

It reminded him of an old story he once heard about the vaults in St. Michan's Church in Dublin—where bodies stay preserved for hundreds of years. Lying in the tub was a thin, gray figure, wrapped in a cloth like a burial shroud. Its lips were curled into a small, creepy smile, and its hands were pressed tightly against its chest.

As Stephen stared, he heard a soft moan. The figure's arms started to move. Fear took over, and he stumbled back—only to wake up and find himself really standing in the hallway, barefoot in the moonlight.

Surprisingly brave for his age, he walked to the bathroom door to see if the figure was real. It wasn't. So he quietly went back to bed.

The next morning, Mrs. Bunch was amazed by his story and even hung up a new curtain over the bathroom window. When Stephen told Mr. Abney about it at breakfast, his cousin seemed very interested. He wrote it down in a notebook he'd been keeping.

Mr. Abney kept talking about the spring equinox and how important it was to ancient people, especially for the young. He reminded Stephen to keep his bedroom window closed at night and mentioned a Roman writer named Censorinus who had smart things to say about it.

Two strange things happened around that time that Stephen never forgot.

The first was after a night when he couldn't sleep well. He didn't remember dreaming, but he felt uneasy the whole time. The next evening, while Mrs. Bunch was helping him with his nightgown, she suddenly said, "Oh my goodness, Master Stephen! How do you manage to tear your nightclothes like this? Just look at it! Do you know how much work this causes for the servants?"

The gown had several long, clean cuts along the left side of the chest—thin slashes about six inches long. Some didn't even go all the way through.

Stephen looked surprised. "I'm sure they weren't there last night," he said. Then added, "But they look a lot like the scratches on the outside of my bedroom door—and I didn't make those."

Mrs. Bunch stared at him in shock, then grabbed a candle and rushed out of the room. A few minutes later, they heard her footsteps going up the stairs.

"Well," she said, "Master Stephen, I just can't figure out how those scratches ended up so high on the door—too high for a cat or dog, and no rat could reach that far either. They looked like the fingernails of a Chinese man, or at least that's what my uncle used to say when we were young. He worked in the tea trade and told us stories like that. If I were you, Master Stephen, I wouldn't tell the master anything about it. Just make sure to lock your door when you go to bed."

"I always do, Mrs. Bunch, right after I say my prayers."

"That's a good boy. Say your prayers, and nothing bad can get to you."

After that, Mrs. Bunch went back to fixing his ripped nightgown, pausing every now and then to think quietly until it was time for bed. That happened on a Friday night in March 1812.

The next evening, something unusual happened. Stephen and Mrs. Bunch were having their usual chat when Mr. Parkes, the butler, suddenly showed up. He normally stayed in his pantry and didn't visit much. He didn't even realize Stephen was there at first. He seemed shaken and was talking faster than usual.

"If Master wants wine in the evening, he can go get it himself," he said. "I'll only go into that cellar during the day now. I don't know what's down there—maybe it's just rats, or maybe the wind got in—but I'm not as young as I used to be, and I can't handle it anymore."

"Well, Mr. Parkes, you know this place does have a lot of rats," Mrs. Bunch replied.

"I'm not saying it doesn't," he said. "And I've heard sailors talk about a rat that could speak—never believed it before. But tonight… if I had put my ear to the door of that far bin, I think I could've made out what they were saying."

"Oh, Mr. Parkes, I don't have time for this nonsense! Rats talking in the wine cellar?"

"I'm not trying to argue, Mrs. Bunch. All I'm saying is—go to the far bin and listen at the door. You might hear it for yourself."

"You really do talk nonsense sometimes, Mr. Parkes. That's no story to tell with children around—you'll scare Master Stephen half to death!"

"What? Master Stephen?" Parkes said, finally realizing Stephen was there. "He knows when I'm just joking around with you."

But Stephen wasn't so sure Parkes had been joking at all. Something about the way he spoke made Stephen uneasy, and even though he asked lots of questions, the butler wouldn't explain anything more about what had happened in the cellar.

Now it was March 24, 1812. It turned out to be a strange day for Stephen. The wind howled all day, shaking the house and the garden, giving everything a restless feeling. As Stephen stood near the fence and looked into the park, it felt like invisible people were rushing past him—caught in the wind, trying to stop, trying to grab onto something to bring them back to the world they had left behind.

After lunch, Mr. Abney said, "Stephen, my boy, could you come see me in my study tonight around eleven o'clock? I'll be busy until then, but there's something very important I want to show you— something about your future. Don't mention it to Mrs. Bunch or anyone else. Just go to your room like usual."

Stephen was thrilled—he loved the idea of staying up late. On his way upstairs that night, he peeked into the library and saw the brazier (which he'd seen before in the corner) now placed in front of the fire. On the table was a silver-gold cup filled with red wine and some pages of writing nearby. Mr. Abney was sprinkling incense into the brazier from a small silver container. He didn't notice Stephen pass by.

Later that night, around ten, the wind had stopped. The moon was full, and everything outside was quiet. Stephen stood by his bedroom window, looking out at the moonlit land. Even though the night seemed calm, strange cries still echoed from the woods. The sounds didn't quite match owls or water birds. They seemed to be getting closer. Soon they weren't coming from the far side of the water anymore—they were right in the garden's shrubs. Then everything went silent.

Stephen was just about to close the window and return to reading Robinson Crusoe when he saw something. Two figures stood on the gravel path below the house—a boy and a girl. They were side by side, looking up at the windows. The girl looked hauntingly familiar, reminding him of the figure he had seen in his dream, lying in the bathtub. But it was the boy who filled him with sudden, sharp fear.

The girl stayed still, gently smiling with her hands resting over her heart. The boy beside her was thin, with messy black hair and worn-out clothes. He lifted his arms high, and something about the way he stood felt threatening—like he was starving for something he could never have. The moonlight lit up his hands, and they looked almost see-through. His fingernails were so long they looked unnatural. As he held his arms up, Stephen noticed something terrifying: a large, dark opening on the left side of the boy's chest. It wasn't exactly a sound, but more like a feeling that hit Stephen's mind—like the sad, desperate cries he'd heard drifting through the woods earlier that night.

Then, without making a sound, the two figures slid across the gravel and disappeared.

Stephen was shaking with fear, but he knew it was nearly time to meet Mr. Abney. He grabbed his candle and hurried downstairs to the study. The door was just off the main hall, and he reached it quickly, driven by panic. He didn't think it was locked—the key was still in the usual spot on the outside. He knocked several times, but no one answered. He could hear Mr. Abney talking inside. Something about his voice made Stephen want to shout out—but when he tried, nothing came. It was like something had frozen the words in his throat. Maybe

Mr. Abney had seen the ghostly children too? Then the room went silent. Stephen shoved at the door, and it finally swung open.

Later, when Stephen was older, he found some papers in the study that explained everything. The most important parts said:

"People from long ago believed that through certain rituals—ones that might seem cruel today—a person could unlock great spiritual power. They thought you could gain control over invisible forces by taking the energy or essence from other humans.

"One man, Simon Magus, was said to have learned how to fly, become invisible, and change shape by using the soul of a young boy. Some claimed he killed the boy to do it. In old writings by Hermes Trismegistus, it says that absorbing the hearts of at least three people under the age of twenty-one could bring about similar powers.

"I've spent the last twenty years testing this idea. I chose people who could disappear without causing much trouble. The first was Phoebe Stanley, a girl with gypsy roots, taken on March 24, 1792. Then there was Giovanni Paoli, a traveling Italian boy, taken on the night of March 23, 1805. The final person I need—though I hate using the word 'victim'—is my cousin, Stephen Elliott. His time must come on March 24, 1812.

"The best way to complete the ritual is to take the heart while the person is still alive, burn it into ash, and mix those ashes with red wine—port is best. The first two bodies should be hidden well, maybe in an old bathroom or the wine cellar. There might be problems caused by the spirits of those taken—what most people call ghosts—but anyone calm and determined enough for this kind of work won't be bothered by them. I'm excited for the powerful new life this ritual could give me. If it works, I'll not only avoid punishment, but maybe even beat death itself."

They found Mr. Abney still sitting in his chair, his head leaning back, his face frozen in a mix of rage, fear, and pain. A deep, torn wound on his left side revealed his heart. There was no blood on his hands, and the long knife on the table was completely clean. It looked like a wild animal had attacked him. The window was open, and the coroner said some kind of creature had gotten in and killed him.

But after reading those papers, Stephen knew the truth was something else entirely.

The Mezzotint

Not too long ago, I told you a story about something strange that happened to a friend of mine named Dennistoun. He was traveling through Europe looking for artwork to bring back to the museum at Cambridge.

When he got home to England, he didn't go around sharing the details of what happened. Still, enough people found out—especially one man who was running an art museum at another university. Since he worked in a similar field as Dennistoun, the story stuck with him. He was eager to believe anything that made the whole thing sound unlikely, because he really didn't want to imagine facing a situation like that himself. Luckily for him, it wasn't his job to search for ancient manuscripts—that responsibility belonged to the Shelburnian Library. They could dig through old corners of Europe for rare texts if they wanted. He was happy to stick to his current task: growing his museum's amazing collection of drawings and prints showing old English towns and buildings.

But as he would soon find out, even a calm and familiar area like topographical art could have its own dark secrets. And Mr. Williams was about to stumble into one.

Anyone with even a small interest in collecting topographical art knows there's one London dealer you can't ignore: Mr. J. W. Britnell. He regularly puts out excellent catalogs filled with engravings, maps, and old drawings of mansions, churches, and towns across England and Wales. These catalogs were like a guidebook for Mr. Williams. Since his museum already owned a huge collection, he didn't usually buy a lot. Still, he kept an eye out for pieces that could fill small gaps in the collection—he didn't expect to find anything rare.

In February of last year, a new catalog from Mr. Britnell showed up on Mr. Williams's desk at the museum. It came with a typed letter from the dealer that said:

DEAR SIR,

We'd like to draw your attention to item No. 978 in the attached catalog, which we'd be happy to send for your review.

Yours truly,

J. W. BRITNELL

Mr. Williams flipped to the listing for No. 978 right away. Here's what it said:

978. — Unknown. An interesting mezzotint: view of a manor house, early 1800s. 15 by 10 inches, black frame. £2 2s.

It didn't sound all that exciting, and the price seemed a bit steep. Still, since Mr. Britnell clearly thought it was worth pointing out—and knew what kind of pieces Mr. Williams usually liked—he decided to request it on approval, along with a few other engravings and sketches from the same catalog.

He didn't give it much more thought after that and went on with the rest of his workday.

Of course, packages always seem to arrive later than expected, and this one was no different. It didn't get to the museum until Saturday afternoon, after Mr. Williams had already left for the day. So, one of the museum staff took it to his college rooms instead, so he wouldn't have to wait until Monday to go through it.

That's where he found it waiting for him when he came home to have tea—with a friend.

The only item that really caught my attention was the large mezzotint in a black frame—the same one I mentioned earlier from Mr. Britnell's catalog. I'll have to describe it in more detail, though I doubt I can explain it as clearly as I see it in my own memory. It looked almost exactly like the kind of old picture you might still find hanging in the hallways of quiet country houses or the sitting rooms of old inns. The print wasn't great quality, and mezzotints like this—especially the bad ones—tend to be the least impressive type of engraving.

The image showed the front of an old manor house, probably from the 1700s. It wasn't very large and had three rows of plain windows, all surrounded by stonework. On top of the house was a flat ledge with decorative balls or vases at the corners. There was a small porch in the center, trees on both sides, and a wide stretch of grass in front. The engraving had the words A. W. F. sculpsit etched into the bottom edge, but no other title or description. It looked like something done by an amateur.

Mr. Williams couldn't understand why Mr. Britnell would ask £2 2s for it. He picked it up with little interest. On the back, there was a torn label. Only parts of two lines were left. The first ended in –ngley Hall, and the second ended in –ssex. He figured it might be worth figuring out exactly which place this was, something he could do with a gazetteer. Then he planned to send it back to Britnell with a note questioning the dealer's judgment.

He lit a few candles—since it had gotten dark—made some tea, and shared it with a friend who had joined him after a round of golf. (Apparently, even the professors at this university found time for golf now and then.) As they drank their tea, they talked about the game—

what shots could've been better and how they hadn't exactly been lucky. Typical golfer talk, really.

While they were chatting, the friend—let's call him Professor Binks—picked up the framed picture and asked, "What place is this, Williams?"

"That's exactly what I'm trying to figure out," Williams said, reaching for the gazetteer. "Check the back. It says something like '–ngley Hall,' maybe in Sussex or Essex. Part of the name's missing. Do you happen to know it?"

"This is from Britnell, right?" Binks asked. "Is it for the museum?"

"Well, I might buy it if it cost five shillings," Williams said. "But he's asking two guineas for it, which is just ridiculous. It's a terrible print, and there aren't even any people in it to make it interesting."

"I don't think it's that bad," Binks replied. "I kind of like the moonlight in the scene. And I do see a figure—maybe just one—down in the front corner."

"Really? Let me see," said Williams. "Hmm, you're right. The lighting is done well. And yes, there's something there—just a head, really—way off to the front edge of the picture."

Sure enough, there it was. Barely more than a dark smudge, it looked like the head of someone bundled in heavy clothing, facing the house with their back turned to the viewer. Williams hadn't noticed it before.

"Okay," he admitted, "it's a little better than I thought. Still, I can't justify spending museum money on a picture of a place I can't even name."

Soon after that, Professor Binks left to go do some work. Williams stayed behind and kept trying to figure out where the house in the picture was from. He wasn't having much luck. "If only that one missing vowel before the 'ng' was still there," he thought. "Then I could figure it out easily." But as it was, the name could be anything— Guestingley, Langley, or something else entirely. "There are more places ending in '–ngley' than I expected," he thought, frustrated. "And this useless book doesn't even have an index for place name endings."

Dinner at Mr. Williams's college, known as Hall, began at seven. There's no need to describe it in detail, especially since it mainly involved casual talk between colleagues who had played golf that afternoon. The conversation wasn't important to the story—just the usual golf banter.

After dinner, Williams likely spent an hour or so in the common room. Later that evening, a few people came back to his rooms. They probably played cards and smoked for a while. During a quiet moment, Williams grabbed the mezzotint from the table without thinking and handed it to someone who had a mild interest in art. He briefly explained where it came from and what little he knew about it.

The man looked at the picture, then said with some curiosity, "This is actually a really nice piece, Williams. It feels like it's from the romantic period. The lighting is done really well, and even though the figure is kind of creepy, it's oddly powerful."

"Yes, isn't it?" Williams replied, though he was busy fixing drinks for the others and didn't walk over to look at the picture again.

By this time, it was getting late, and the guests began to leave. After they were gone, Williams had to write a couple of letters and wrap up some tasks. It wasn't until after midnight that he finally got ready for bed. He lit his bedroom candle and turned off the lamp. The picture was still lying face-up on the table, just where the last guest had left it. As Williams dimmed the light, his eyes landed on the engraving—and what he saw nearly made him drop the candle.

He later said that if the room had gone dark at that moment, he might've passed out. But the light stayed on, so he managed to set the candle down and stare closely at the picture. What he saw was impossible—completely unbelievable—but it was real. A figure had appeared on the lawn in front of the house. It hadn't been there earlier that day, when he first looked at the image around five o'clock.

Now, the figure was crawling on all fours toward the house. It wore a long, dark cloak, and on its back was a white cross.

Williams wasn't sure what the right thing to do was in a situation like this. But here's what he did: he picked up the picture by one corner and carried it across the hallway to a second set of rooms he owned. He locked it in a drawer, secured both rooms, and got ready for bed. Before sleeping, he wrote and signed a note describing what he had seen and how the image had changed since it arrived.

He didn't fall asleep right away, but it helped to know that he wasn't the only one who'd noticed something odd. One of his guests had seen something strange in the picture too. If that hadn't been the case, Williams might have thought he was losing his mind. But now that he knew he wasn't imagining it, he had two things to do the next day: take a closer look at the mezzotint—with a witness—and figure out where the house in the image actually was.

He decided to invite his neighbor Nisbet over for breakfast and spend the morning searching through the gazetteer for clues.

Nisbet was free and arrived around 9:30. Williams, unfortunately, was still getting dressed when he showed up. During breakfast,

Williams didn't say much about the mezzotint, other than mentioning he had a picture he wanted Nisbet to look at. Those who've lived the university life can probably imagine the kind of wide-ranging conversation the two Fellows of Canterbury College had that morning—everything from golf to tennis was on the table.

Still, Williams was clearly distracted. His thoughts kept drifting back to the strange engraving now sitting face-down in a drawer across the hall.

Finally, once the morning smoke break began, the moment he had been waiting for arrived. Feeling nervous and excited, he hurried across to his other room, unlocked the drawer, carefully picked up the picture—still turned over—and brought it back, placing it in Nisbet's hands.

"Alright," said Williams, "Nisbet, I want you to look at the picture carefully and describe everything you see. Be as detailed as you can. I'll explain why afterward."

Nisbet studied it for a moment. "Well, it's a view of a country house—looks like it's in England—at night under the moon."

"You're sure it's moonlight?" Williams asked.

"Absolutely. The moon looks like it's in its last phase, and there are clouds in the sky."

"Okay, go on," Williams said. Under his breath, he muttered, "There was no moon the first time I saw it."

"There's not much more to say," Nisbet continued. "The house has three rows of windows—five in each row. The middle window on the ground floor is replaced with a small porch. And—"

"What about people?" Williams asked, clearly interested.

"There aren't any," said Nisbet. "But—"

"What? No one on the lawn?"

"Nope, no one."

"You're absolutely sure?"

"Totally. But I did notice something else."

"What is it?"

"One of the windows on the ground floor, to the left of the front door, is open."

"Seriously? Then he must have gotten inside," said Williams, clearly alarmed. He hurried around to see the picture for himself. It was true— the figure was gone, and now one of the windows was open. Williams stood frozen for a second, then rushed to his desk and began writing something down.

He returned with two sheets of paper. He asked Nisbet to sign one—it was the written description Nisbet had just given—and then handed him the second, which was Williams's own account from the night before.

"What do you think is going on here?" Nisbet asked.

"That's the big question," said Williams. "There are three things I need to do now. First, I have to ask Garwood"—that was the guest who had seen the picture the previous night—"what he remembers. Then I need to get this image photographed before anything else changes. And last, I have to figure out where this house actually is."

"I can take care of the photo," said Nisbet. "But this really feels like we're witnessing something tragic unfold. The only question is whether it already happened or is about to happen. You definitely need to identify that house. And yes, I think you're right—he's probably inside now. If I had to guess, something terrible is about to happen upstairs."

"I'll take the picture to old Green," Williams said. Green was the most senior professor at the college and had managed the school's properties for many years. "He might know the place. The college owns land in both Essex and Sussex, and he's probably visited both areas."

"Good idea," said Nisbet. "But let me take a photo first. Although, I think Green's away today. He wasn't at dinner last night, and I'm pretty sure he said he was leaving for the weekend."

"You're right," said Williams. "He went to Brighton. Okay, take the picture now, and I'll go speak with Garwood and ask what he saw. Keep an eye on the mezzotint while I'm gone. Honestly, I'm starting to think two guineas was a fair price after all."

Soon after, Williams came back—this time with Garwood. Garwood explained that when he saw the figure, it had just moved away from the edge of the image and hadn't gone far onto the lawn. He remembered a white mark on its back but wasn't sure if it was a cross. Williams wrote it down, and Garwood signed it. Then Nisbet went ahead and took a photograph of the mezzotint.

"So, what's the plan now?" Nisbet asked. "Are you just going to keep watching it all day?"

"No, I don't think that's necessary," said Williams. "I have a feeling we're supposed to see the whole thing play out. A lot of time passed between last night and this morning, and all that changed was that the figure entered the house. If it had finished whatever it came to do, the window might've been closed again. But since it's still open, I think it's still inside. That makes me think nothing will change during the day."

He continued, "We could go out for a walk this afternoon, then come back for tea—or once it gets dark. I'll leave the picture out on the table and lock the room. My housekeeper can still get in, but no one else will."

The three of them agreed it was a solid plan. They also thought it would be smart to stick together for the afternoon so they wouldn't accidentally tell anyone what was happening. If word got out, the Phasmatological Society—known for investigating ghost stories and supernatural things—would be all over them.

So we'll leave them there for now, until five o'clock.

Around five o'clock, the three men returned to Williams's rooms. At first, they were a little annoyed to see the door hadn't been locked. Then they remembered it was Sunday, and on Sundays the servants came by earlier than usual to take instructions. But what they found inside took them completely by surprise.

The picture was still sitting on the table, leaning against a stack of books, just as they had left it. But opposite it, sitting in a chair and staring at it in shock, was Williams's servant. His name was Mr. Filcher (not made up), and he was known for being very proper. He had worked at the college a long time and set the standard for good behavior—not just in their college, but in others nearby. It was totally unlike him to sit in his employer's chair, or to take any personal interest in his master's belongings. He clearly knew this himself. When the three men walked in, he jumped to his feet like he'd been caught doing something wrong.

"I'm sorry, sir," he said quickly. "I shouldn't have sat down without permission."

"No worries, Robert," Williams replied. "Actually, I was going to ask what you thought of that picture."

"Well, sir," the man said, "I wouldn't hang it where my little girl could see it."

"You wouldn't? Why not?"

"She once saw a Bible with pictures that were nothing like this one—and we had to stay up with her three or four nights after that. If she saw that skeleton, or whatever it is, carrying off the poor baby, she'd be terrified. You know how kids are—how jumpy they get over the smallest things. I just don't think it's the kind of picture that should be left out, not where someone could walk in and get a scare."

"Will you need anything else this evening, sir? Thank you." And with that, Mr. Filcher continued his rounds.

As soon as he left, the three men rushed over to the picture. The house was still there under the dim moonlight and drifting clouds. The window that had been open was now closed. The figure had returned to the lawn, but this time it wasn't crawling. It was standing upright and walking quickly—taking long strides toward the front of the image.

The moonlight shone from behind, and the dark cloak it wore hung down over its face, hiding most of it. What little they could see was enough to make them glad the rest was covered. Just a pale forehead and a few scraggly strands of hair were visible beneath the hood. Its head was bowed, and its arms were wrapped tightly around something. It was hard to see clearly, but they could just make out the shape of a child. Whether the child was alive or not, they couldn't tell. Only the creature's legs were clearly visible, and they were disturbingly thin.

From five until seven, the three men took turns watching the picture, hoping for more changes. But it stayed exactly the same.

Eventually, they agreed it was probably safe to leave it alone again and planned to check back after dinner to see what might happen next.

When they returned later that evening—as soon as they could—the picture was still there. But the figure was gone. The house sat quietly under the moonlight, just like before. With nothing else to do, they decided to spend the evening digging through guidebooks and gazetteers, hoping to figure out the location of the house in the image.

At 11:30 p.m., Williams finally got lucky. He was reading from Murray's Guide to Essex when he found this entry:

16½ miles, Anningley. The church was originally Norman, but was redesigned in a more classical style in the 1700s. It holds the tomb of the Francis family. Their home, Anningley Hall, is a sturdy Queen Anne house located just past the churchyard in a park of about 80 acres. The family line ended after the last heir mysteriously vanished as a baby in 1802. The father, Arthur Francis, was known in the area as a skilled amateur mezzotint engraver. After his son disappeared, he lived alone at the Hall and was found dead in his studio exactly three years later. He had just completed an engraving of the house, which is now extremely rare.

This felt like a breakthrough. When Mr. Green returned, he confirmed it: the house in the picture was definitely Anningley Hall.

"Do you know anything about that figure in the image, Green?" Williams asked.

"I'm not sure," Green replied. "But here's what people used to say when I first heard about it—before I came to the college. Old Mr. Francis was known for being really hard on poachers. Anytime he thought someone was hunting illegally on his land, he'd find a way to get them kicked off. Over time, he got rid of all of them—except one.

"Back then, landowners could get away with a lot more than they can today. The last man left was from a very old family—used to be Lords of the Manor, I believe. We had a similar case in my own hometown."

"You mean like that guy in Tess of the D'Urbervilles?" Williams asked.

"Yeah, probably," Green replied. "I've never been able to finish that book myself. But this man—Gawdy, that was his name—he could point out a row of family tombs in the church and claim them as his ancestors. That kind of thing made him bitter, I think. Still, Francis couldn't touch him. Gawdy always stayed just within the law—until one night, the gamekeepers caught him poaching in a wood at the far edge of the estate. I can still show you the exact spot—it borders land my uncle used to own.

"You can imagine the fight that followed. Gawdy, unlucky man, ended up shooting one of the keepers. That's all Francis needed. The grand jury—well, they weren't hard to convince back then—and Gawdy was hanged not long after. I've even been shown the place where he was buried, on the north side of the church. You know how it is in that part of the country: people who are hanged or take their own lives are always buried on the north side.

"The story goes that someone close to Gawdy—not a relative, because he didn't have any—decided to get revenge by taking Francis's son, ending the Francis family line. I don't know—it seems like a pretty extreme idea for a poacher from Essex. But now... I wouldn't be surprised if it was Gawdy himself who pulled it off. Ugh, I hate even thinking about it. Here, have some whisky, Williams."

Williams later shared everything with Dennistoun, who told the story to a group that included me and a skeptical professor of

Ophiology. When someone asked the professor what he thought, all he said was, "Oh, those Bridgeford people will believe anything." That comment got the reaction it deserved.

One final note: the picture is now in the Ashleian Museum. Experts have tested it to see if invisible ink or anything like that was used, but nothing turned up. Mr. Britnell, the dealer, didn't know anything about its background—only that it was rare. Since then, the picture has been closely watched, but it has never changed again.

The Ash-Tree

If you've ever traveled through eastern England, you've probably seen the small country houses scattered across the land. They're usually a bit gloomy, built in an Italian style, and set in parks that are about 80 to 100 acres wide. I've always found these places interesting—the faded wooden fences, tall old trees, quiet ponds surrounded by reeds, and the line of trees in the distance.

I especially like the ones with big columns at the front, often added to a red-brick Queen Anne-style house. These houses were usually covered in plaster later on to match the "Grecian" style that became popular in the late 1700s. Inside, there's usually a high-ceilinged hallway with a balcony and a small organ—I think every house like that should have one. The libraries are also amazing. You might find anything from a religious book from the 1200s to a rare old copy of Shakespeare. I enjoy the paintings too, of course. But what I love most is imagining what it was like to live there when the house was brand new—back when rich landowners lived in luxury. And even today, when money is tighter, there's still something special about these places. Honestly, I'd love to own a house like that someday—just enough money to care for it and invite friends over sometimes.

But I'm getting off track. I need to tell you about something strange that happened at one of these houses. It's called Castringham Hall, and it's in Suffolk. The house has been updated over the years, but many of the original features are still there: the Italian-style columns, the square white walls that look newer than the inside really is, the trees along the edge of the park, and the pond.

There used to be one unusual thing that made Castringham stand out. If you looked at it from the front, you'd see a huge ash tree growing just a few yards from the house. Its branches were so close they touched the building. That tree had probably been there since the estate stopped being a fortified area—when the moat was filled in and the current house was built during Elizabethan times. By 1690, the tree had reached its full size.

That year, the area around Castringham was caught up in a wave of witch trials. It's still hard to understand what made people back then so terrified of witches. Did the accused really believe they had powers? Were they just angry enough to want to hurt others? Or were their confessions forced out by cruel witch-hunters? No one really knows, and the story I'm about to tell makes the truth even harder to figure out. I can't say if it's all made up. You'll have to decide for yourself.

Castringham played a part in this chapter of history. The accused witch was a woman named Mrs. Mothersole. She wasn't poor like most of the others accused—she actually had some money and influence in the village. A few well-known farmers tried to defend her. They spoke up for her and were very nervous about how the jury would decide.

But the testimony that ruined her chances came from the owner of Castringham Hall, a man named Sir Matthew Fell. He said that on three different nights, each during a full moon, he had seen her from his window collecting branches from the ash tree near his home. According to him, she was wearing just a nightgown and used a curved knife to cut off small twigs while muttering to herself. Each time, he tried to catch her, but she always heard a noise he made and ran away. When he got outside, all he ever saw was a hare racing toward the village.

On the third night, Sir Matthew made a serious effort to catch Mrs. Mothersole. He followed as fast as he could and went straight to her house. When he got there, he spent about fifteen minutes banging on her door. She finally answered, looking annoyed and half-asleep, like she had just gotten out of bed. She clearly hadn't been expecting him, and he didn't have a good reason for showing up.

Her strange actions near the ash tree became the strongest evidence at her trial. Other people from the village also gave statements, but none were as unusual or convincing as Sir Matthew's. Because of what he said, Mrs. Mothersole was found guilty of witchcraft and sentenced to death. A week later, she was hanged along with five or six others in Bury St. Edmunds.

Sir Matthew, who was Deputy-Sheriff at the time, was there to witness the execution. It was a cold, wet morning in March when the cart carrying the prisoners climbed the grassy hill outside Northgate, where the gallows stood. Most of the people being hanged looked numb or broken, but Mrs. Mothersole stood out. Even at the end, she seemed fierce and strong. A writer at the time said her "poisonous rage" was so intense that it even shook the crowd—and the hangman. People said she looked possessed, almost like a living demon. She didn't fight back, but the way she stared at the officers was so terrifying that one of them later admitted the memory haunted him for six months.

The only words she spoke were strange and quiet: "There will be guests at the Hall." She said this more than once in a low voice, and no one understood what it meant.

Sir Matthew was clearly disturbed by everything that happened. On the way home, he talked about it with the local vicar. He hadn't wanted to testify, but he truly believed what he saw and insisted he wasn't mistaken. The whole experience had deeply unsettled him—he was someone who preferred to keep peace with those around him—but he believed he had done what was right. The vicar, Mr. Crome, agreed.

A few weeks later, under a full moon in May, the two men met again and went for a walk in the park, eventually ending up at Castringham Hall. Lady Fell was away taking care of her sick mother, so Sir Matthew was alone. He invited Mr. Crome to stay for a late supper.

That evening, Sir Matthew didn't talk much. Most of their conversation was about local news and family matters. At one point, he wrote down some notes about his wishes for the estate—notes that would later prove important.

When Mr. Crome was about to leave around 9:30, they took a short walk behind the house. As they passed the big ash tree near the windows, Sir Matthew suddenly stopped.

"What's that climbing up and down the tree trunk?" he asked. "It can't be a squirrel—they're all in their nests by now."

Mr. Crome looked and saw something moving, but he couldn't tell its color in the moonlight. However, he caught a quick, clear glimpse of its shape, and though it sounded silly, he swore later that whatever it was had more than four legs.

The moment passed quickly, and the strange figure disappeared. The two men said goodbye. If they ever saw each other again, it wasn't for another twenty years.

The next morning, Sir Matthew didn't come downstairs at six like usual. He wasn't there at seven, or even by eight. The servants became concerned and knocked on his bedroom door. There's no need to explain how their worry grew. Eventually, they opened the door—

from the outside—and found Sir Matthew dead. His body was cold and darkened. You may have already guessed that.

At first, there were no clear signs of what caused his death. But the bedroom window was wide open.

One of the servants went to get the vicar, and then, following his instructions, rode off to inform the coroner. Mr. Crome, the vicar, rushed to the Hall and was shown to the room where Sir Matthew's body lay. In his personal notes, he wrote about how deeply respected and mourned Sir Matthew was. He also included a passage that sheds some light on what happened—and on what people believed at the time:

"There was no sign that anyone had broken into the room. But the window was open, which Sir Matthew always insisted on during that season. His usual evening drink—light ale in a silver cup—was still sitting on the bedside table, untouched. The doctor from Bury, a Mr. Hodgkins, tested the drink and later swore under oath at the coroner's inquest that he found no trace of poison. Still, because the body had turned black and swollen, the neighbors couldn't help but suspect poisoning.

"The body was twisted in a strange and awful way, as if Sir Matthew had died in terrible pain. And something even stranger happened. The two women assigned to prepare and clean the body—both experienced and well-respected in their work—came to me deeply upset. They said that the moment they touched Sir Matthew's chest with their bare hands, they felt an intense burning and aching in their palms. Their forearms also began to swell badly, and the pain didn't go away. They ended up being unable to work for several weeks—even though no marks showed on their skin.

"After hearing this, I brought the doctor back and, using a small magnifying glass, we carefully examined that part of the skin. We didn't find anything unusual except for two tiny punctures, like needle marks. We guessed that poison might have entered through those spots. It reminded us of stories about the ring used by Pope Borgia, and other cases of secret poisoning by Italians in the past.

"That's everything we could confirm about the condition of the body. What I'm about to share next is just a personal experiment, and I leave it to the future to decide if it's meaningful or not.

"Next to the bed was a small Bible, which Sir Matthew used to read from every morning and night. Holding it, and thinking sadly of my lost friend, I suddenly remembered an old tradition—some might call it superstition—of using random Bible verses for guidance in times of need. This method, known as Sortes, had once been used by King Charles I and Lord Falkland, and people still spoke of it. I admit, I didn't find much help in what I read. But in case someone someday understands more than I do, I'll share the results.

"I tried three times, opening the book and pointing to a verse. The first was Luke 13:7: 'Cut it down.' The second, Isaiah 13:20: 'It shall never be inhabited.' The third was Job 39:30: 'Her young ones also suck up blood.'"

That's all that needs to be said from Mr. Crome's notes. Sir Matthew Fell was properly buried, and Mr. Crome gave a sermon at the funeral the following Sunday. The sermon was later printed under the title "The Unsearchable Way; or, England's Danger and the Malicious Dealings of Antichrist." The vicar, like many others in the area, believed that Sir Matthew had been murdered as part of a renewed threat from the so-called Popish Plot.

His son, also named Sir Matthew, inherited the title and the estate. And with that, the first part of the strange story of Castringham comes to an end. It's worth noting—though not surprising—that the new baronet refused to sleep in the room where his father had died. In fact, almost no one used that room again except for an occasional visitor. Sir Matthew the second died in 1735. Nothing unusual seemed to happen during his time—except for one odd detail: his cattle and other animals started dying more often than normal, and the problem slowly got worse over the years.

Anyone who's curious about the details can find a full report in a letter sent to the Gentleman's Magazine in 1772. The writer used information taken directly from the baronet's own papers. He finally solved the problem with a simple fix—he had all his animals locked up in sheds at night and stopped keeping sheep in the park. He'd noticed that nothing bad ever happened to animals that slept indoors. After that, whatever was causing the strange deaths only seemed to affect wild birds and game animals. But since no one could describe clear symptoms, and watching the animals overnight never revealed anything useful, people stopped talking much about what the local farmers had come to call "the Castringham sickness."

The second Sir Matthew died in 1735, as already mentioned, and his son, Sir Richard, inherited everything. During his time, a large family pew was added to the north side of the church. His plans were so grand that several old graves on that side had to be dug up. One of them belonged to Mrs. Mothersole, and her exact burial spot was known thanks to a map of the churchyard drawn by Mr. Crome.

Word spread quickly through the village that the grave of the infamous witch would be opened, and people were curious. When the coffin was found, everyone was shocked. It was still sealed and in good condition, but it was completely empty—no body, no bones, not even dust. This was especially strange because, at the time she was buried, no one worried about grave robbers. And there wouldn't have been any reason to steal a body except for use in a medical school, which seemed unlikely here.

The discovery brought back old stories about witch trials and magic that had been forgotten for forty years. When Sir Richard ordered the coffin to be burned, many people thought it was a foolish and risky move—but the order was carried out anyway.

Sir Richard was clearly a man who liked to change things. Before his time, Castringham Hall had been a beautiful red-brick house. But Sir Richard had traveled in Italy, and after falling in love with the Italian style, he decided to turn the Hall into something like a palace. He had the red bricks covered in plaster and stone, added cheap Roman statues to the hall and garden, and even built a copy of the Sibyl's Temple from Tivoli across the pond. Castringham looked completely different— some thought it was less charming, but others admired it, and several local landowners copied the style in the years that followed.

Then, one morning in 1754, Sir Richard woke up after a very rough night. The wind had been strong, his fireplace kept filling the room with smoke, but it was too cold to go without a fire. Something also kept rattling his window so loudly that he barely slept. On top of all that, he was expecting important guests that day, who would want some hunting or entertainment. Unfortunately, the mysterious illness still affecting the game animals had been so bad recently that he was worried it would ruin his reputation. But more than anything, it was his terrible night's sleep that bothered him. He decided then and there that he couldn't spend another night in that room.

He thought about it all through breakfast, and afterward, he started checking other rooms in the house to find one he liked better. But it took a long time. One room faced east, so the sun would wake him too early. Another faced north, but the servants were always walking past it. One had a bed he didn't like. He finally decided he needed a room that faced west—so the sun wouldn't wake him—and that was out of the way, where he wouldn't be disturbed. The housekeeper, Mrs. Chiddock, was running out of suggestions.

"Well, Sir Richard," she said, "there's really only one room that fits that description."

"And which room is that?" he asked.

"That would be the West Chamber—Sir Matthew's old room."

"Then that's where I'll sleep tonight," Sir Richard said, heading off down the hallway. "Which way is it? Ah yes, over here."

Mrs. Chiddock hurried after him. "Oh, Sir Richard, no one's used that room in forty years. The air hasn't even been aired out since your father died in there."

"Come now, open the door," Sir Richard said. "At least let me see the room."

So she opened it. The air inside was heavy and stale, smelling of earth and dust. Sir Richard walked straight to the window and, as usual with him, threw the shutters wide open and pushed the window open without hesitation. This part of the house hadn't been changed much over the years. The ash tree had grown up right next to it, and thick branches blocked the view.

"Let it air out all day," he said. "Move my bed and furniture in this afternoon. Put the Bishop of Kilmore in my old room."

56

"Excuse me, Sir Richard," said a voice, interrupting, "might I have a moment of your time?"

Sir Richard turned to see a man dressed in black standing at the doorway, giving a polite bow.

"Forgive the interruption, Sir Richard. You may not remember me. My name is William Crome. My grandfather was the vicar here during your grandfather's time."

"Well, Mr. Crome," said Sir Richard, "anyone with the name Crome is always welcome at Castringham. It's good to continue a friendship that's lasted two generations. What can I do for you? You look like you're in a hurry."

"You're right about that, sir. I'm traveling from Norwich to Bury St. Edmunds as fast as I can, but I wanted to stop here to give you some papers we recently found among my grandfather's things. We thought you might find them interesting, especially for your family records."

"That's very kind of you, Mr. Crome. Please come with me to the parlor. We'll have a glass of wine and take a look at the papers together. And you, Mrs. Chiddock, as I said earlier, air out this room. Yes, this is where my grandfather died. And yes, I know the tree makes it a bit damp. No more objections—I've made up my mind. Go ahead now. Mr. Crome, will you follow me?"

They went to the study. The packet William Crome had brought— he had just been made a Fellow at Clare Hall in Cambridge and would later publish a respectable edition of Polyaenus—included, among other things, the notes his grandfather had written after Sir Matthew Fell's death. For the first time, Sir Richard saw the strange Bible verses the old vicar had marked. They amused him.

"Well," said Sir Richard, "my grandfather's Bible gave some solid advice—'Cut it down.' If that means the ash tree, he can rest easy. I'll make sure it's taken care of. That tree's nothing but a breeding ground for coughs and fevers."

The parlor held the family's small book collection, which would later be replaced by a much larger one Sir Richard had gathered in Italy—once he built a proper library.

Sir Richard glanced up from the paper at the bookshelf. "I wonder," he said, "if the old prophet is still there. I think I see him." He walked across the room and pulled out a short, thick Bible. On the inside cover was written: "To Matthew Fell, from his loving godmother, Anne Aldous, 2 September, 1659."

"Maybe we should test it again, Mr. Crome. I bet we'll land on a verse full of names from the Chronicles. Hmm, what have we got here? 'You shall look for me in the morning, but I will not be there.' Well, well! Your grandfather would've thought that was quite the warning, don't you think? No more Bible fortunes for me. They're all nonsense."

He turned back to Mr. Crome. "Anyway, thank you very much for the papers. I'm sure you need to get going. But before you do, let me offer you another glass."

They parted on friendly terms, and Sir Richard truly meant the invitation. He liked the young man's manners and thought well of him.

Later that afternoon, the guests arrived—Bishop of Kilmore, Lady Mary Hervey, Sir William Kentfield, and others. They had dinner at five, followed by wine, card games, supper, and then headed to bed.

The next morning, Sir Richard wasn't interested in going hunting with the rest. Instead, he walked with the Bishop of Kilmore. This bishop, unlike many of his Irish peers, had actually spent time in his parish and knew the people there well. As they walked along the terrace talking about the updates to the house, the Bishop pointed to the window of the West Room.

"No one in my parish would ever sleep in that room," he said.

"Why not, my lord? It's actually my own," replied Sir Richard.

"Well, the people in Ireland believe it brings terrible luck to sleep near an ash tree. And you have one growing just a couple yards from your window. Maybe it's already affected you—you don't look quite as rested as your guests would like to see."

"You're right, my lord. I couldn't sleep from midnight to four. But the tree's coming down tomorrow, so I shouldn't be disturbed much longer."

"That's a wise decision. It can't be healthy to breathe air filtered through all those leaves."

"Exactly. But I didn't even have the window open last night. It was the sound—the constant scratching—I assume from the branches hitting the glass."

"I don't think that's possible, Sir Richard. Look from here. Even the closest branches don't touch the window unless there's a strong wind—and there wasn't one last night. They miss the glass by at least a foot."

"You're right. Then what was it that scratched and rattled the window so much? It even left marks in the dust on the windowsill."

They finally agreed it must've been rats climbing up through the ivy. That was the Bishop's guess, and Sir Richard quickly agreed.

The rest of the day passed quietly. Evening came, the guests went to their rooms, and they all wished Sir Richard a better night's sleep.

Now we're back in his bedroom. The lights are out. Sir Richard is in bed. His room is above the kitchen. The night outside is calm and warm, so he has left the window open.

There wasn't much light near the bed, but something was moving. It looked like Sir Richard's head was shaking back and forth very quickly, and he was making only the faintest sound. But then, in the dim light, it started to seem like there wasn't just one head—but several. Round, brown shapes moved around his shoulders and chest, back and forth. It was a terrible illusion. Or was it real?

Suddenly, something dropped off the bed with a soft thump, like a kitten landing on the floor. It rushed out the open window in a flash. Then another. And another. Four in total. After that, silence.

"You shall seek me in the morning, and I shall not be."

Just like with Sir Matthew, Sir Richard was found dead in his bed— his body blackened and still.

Once the news spread, the guests and servants quietly gathered under his window. People began guessing what had caused his death: poison from Italy, secret Catholic agents, or maybe bad air. The Bishop of Kilmore stared at the ash tree. In the fork of its lower branches, a white tomcat crouched, staring deep into a hollow in the trunk. It seemed to be watching something inside with intense focus.

Suddenly, the cat leaned forward, trying to get a better look. A piece of the edge broke off beneath it, and the cat slipped and tumbled into the hollow. The crash made everyone look up.

Most people know cats can make noise, but few have ever heard the kind of awful sound that came from inside the tree. There were two or three terrible screams—no one could say exactly how many. Then the screaming stopped, replaced by muffled sounds of movement or struggle. Lady Mary Hervey fainted immediately. The housekeeper clamped her hands over her ears and ran until she collapsed on the terrace.

The Bishop and Sir William Kentfield stayed put, but even they were shaken. Though it was "just" a cat's cry, Sir William had to swallow hard before he could say:

"There's something in that tree we don't understand, my lord. We need to find out what it is."

Everyone agreed. They brought a ladder, and one of the gardeners climbed up. He peered into the hollow but couldn't see much—just the faint movement of something inside. They tied a lantern to a rope and slowly lowered it into the trunk.

"We have to get to the bottom of this," said Sir William. "I'd bet my life the cause of these deaths is in that tree."

The gardener climbed back up with the lantern and carefully lowered it again. They saw the glow on his face as he leaned over the opening. Then, his expression changed to one of total shock and horror. He let out a terrible cry, fell backward off the ladder—and luckily, two men caught him before he hit the ground. The lantern fell into the tree.

The gardener had fainted, and it took a while to bring him back around. But by then, something else had happened. The lantern had shattered at the bottom of the tree, and the fire had caught on the dry leaves and debris. Thick smoke poured out, then flames. The ash tree was on fire.

Everyone backed away, forming a circle at a safe distance. Sir William and the Bishop sent people to get weapons and tools.

Whatever had been living inside the tree was going to be forced out by the flames.

And it was.

First, near the base of the tree, they saw something round and flaming—about the size of a person's head—suddenly appear, then drop back inside. This happened several times. Then, one of the burning shapes jumped into the air and landed on the grass. It twitched for a moment, then stopped moving. The Bishop stepped closer and saw what it was—an enormous spider, burned and shriveled, with bulging veins and horrible features.

As the fire burned deeper into the trunk, more of these creatures began to crawl out. Their bodies were covered in grayish hair. The men stood around the tree all day, killing the monsters as they came out. Eventually, none appeared for a long while, and they cautiously moved in to check the base of the tree.

The Bishop later wrote that they found a rounded hollow beneath the roots, like a den. Inside were two or three more of the creatures, already dead from the smoke. But the strangest thing of all was what they found beside them.

Lying against the wall of the hollow was the dried-out body of a person—skin still clinging to the bones, with patches of black hair. Experts later confirmed it was the remains of a woman who had clearly been dead for about fifty years.

Number 13

Viborg is one of the most important towns in Jutland. It's the home of a bishop, has a beautiful but mostly modern cathedral, a lovely park, a scenic lake, and lots of storks. Not far from the town is Hald, known as one of the prettiest places in Denmark. Also nearby is Finderup, where Marsk Stig murdered King Erik Glipping on St. Cecilia's Day in 1286. When the king's tomb was opened in the 1600s, they found fifty-six marks from iron maces on his skull. But I'm not here to write a travel guide.

There are several good hotels in Viborg—Preisler's and the Phœnix are excellent choices. But my cousin, whose story I'm about to share, stayed at the Golden Lion the first time he visited. He never returned, and what happened during that visit will explain why.

The Golden Lion is one of the few buildings in Viborg that survived the big fire of 1726, which destroyed most of the city's older buildings, including the cathedral, the parish church, the town hall, and many other historic spots. The hotel is a large red-brick building with stepped gables and a Bible verse over the front door. Inside the courtyard, where the horse-drawn bus dropped off passengers, the building changes to a half-timbered style with black and white wood and plaster.

The sun was low in the sky when my cousin walked up to the door, and the last light of the day lit up the front of the building. He was immediately impressed by its old-fashioned charm and expected to have an enjoyable and interesting stay in such a classic Jutland inn.

Mr. Anderson, my cousin, wasn't in Viborg for typical business. He was doing research on Denmark's church history and had learned that the Viborg State Archives held some rare documents that had survived the fire. These papers dealt with the final days of Roman Catholicism in the region. He planned to spend up to three weeks studying and copying them. He hoped the Golden Lion had a room large enough to serve as both a bedroom and a study.

He explained all this to the innkeeper, who, after thinking it over, suggested that Mr. Anderson take a look at a few larger rooms and choose the one he liked best. This seemed like a great idea.

The rooms on the top floor were ruled out immediately—too many stairs after a long day of work. The second floor didn't have anything quite the right size. But on the first floor, there were two or three rooms that would work well.

The landlord strongly recommended Room 17, but Mr. Anderson pointed out that its windows faced a blank wall, making it dark in the afternoon. He preferred Room 12 or Room 14, since both looked out onto the street. Even if there was a bit more noise, the evening light and view made up for it.

In the end, he chose Room 12. Like the others, it had three windows on one side. It was fairly tall and unusually long. There was no fireplace, but it had a handsome old stove made of cast iron. On the side of the stove was a carved image of Abraham about to sacrifice Isaac, with the words "1 Book of Moses, Chapter 22" written above. There wasn't much else of interest in the room, except for an old colored print of the town dated around 1820.

Supper was nearly ready, but after freshening up, Mr. Anderson had a few minutes before the bell rang. He used the time to check the list of other guests. As was common in Denmark, the names were written on a large blackboard divided by room numbers. The list wasn't very exciting. There was a lawyer, a German, and a few salesmen from Copenhagen. But one thing did catch his attention—there was no Room 13 on the board.

He had seen this before in other Danish hotels, but it still made him curious. He wondered if people really avoided that number so often that it was hard to rent out a room labeled 13. He decided he would ask the innkeeper if hotel owners had actually had problems convincing guests to stay in a Room 13.

He didn't tell me anything about dinner that night—there wasn't much to say—and he spent the rest of the evening unpacking and organizing his clothes, books, and papers. Nothing unusual happened. Around eleven, he decided to go to bed. But like many people, he couldn't fall asleep unless he read a few pages of something first. He remembered that the book he'd been reading on the train—and the only one he felt like reading—was in the pocket of his overcoat, which he'd left hanging on a hook outside the dining room.

He went downstairs to grab it. The hallways were well-lit, so it was easy to find his way back. At least, that's what he thought. But when he tried to open his room door, the handle wouldn't turn, and he heard someone moving quickly inside. Clearly, it wasn't his room. Had he gone too far to the right or left?

He checked the number: 13.

His room must be next door to the left—and it was. Once inside, he got into bed, read his usual few pages, turned out the light, and settled in. But as he lay there, it struck him: the hotel's room list hadn't included a Number 13. And yet, there it was—right next to his room. He wished now that he'd chosen that room himself. It might have helped the landlord rent it more easily in the future—he could say a well-mannered Englishman had stayed there for weeks and liked it. Still, the room was probably used for storage or staff. It likely wasn't as large or as nice as his own.

Looking around in the dim glow from the streetlight outside, he noticed something odd. Rooms usually look bigger in low light, but this one felt like it had shrunk in length and grown taller. Still, sleep was more important than overthinking—and soon enough, he drifted off.

The next day, Anderson went to the Viborg State Archives. As you'd expect in Denmark, he was warmly welcomed, and everything he needed was made easily available. To his surprise, the documents were even more numerous and fascinating than he'd expected. In addition to official papers, he found a thick bundle of letters about Bishop Jörgen Friis, the last Catholic bishop of the area. These letters revealed lots of personal stories and gossip from the time.

One name kept coming up—a man who lived in a house the Bishop owned in town. The Bishop didn't live there himself, but the man who did caused a scandal. The Protestant writers called him a disgrace to the town. They said he practiced dark and evil arts and had sold his soul to the devil. They blamed the Bishop for protecting someone like that and said it showed how corrupt and superstitious the Catholic Church had become.

The Bishop responded firmly, saying he hated anything to do with magic or secret practices. He challenged his critics to take the matter to the Church court and promised to punish the man—whose name was Mag Nicolas Francken—if the evidence proved he was guilty.

Anderson didn't have time to read much of the next letter, which was from a Protestant leader named Rasmus Nielsen, before the archive closed for the day. But he got the general idea: Nielsen was saying that Christians no longer had to listen to decisions from Catholic bishops. The Bishop's court, he argued, wasn't fit to judge something so serious.

When Anderson left the building, he walked with the head archivist, Herr Scavenius. Naturally, they talked about the letters. While Scavenius was very familiar with most of the documents in the archives, he wasn't an expert on the Reformation. He was interested in what Anderson had found and said he looked forward to reading the book Anderson planned to write.

He added, "I've always been puzzled about where Bishop Friis's town house was. I've studied old maps of Viborg carefully, but it's unfortunate—the section of the Bishop's 1560 property record that listed his town buildings is missing. Maybe I'll still find it someday."

Later, after getting some fresh air—Anderson didn't mention how—he returned to the Golden Lion for supper, a few rounds of solitaire, and then went to bed.

On the way to his room, he remembered that he'd meant to ask the landlord why there was no Room 13 listed on the board. But before bringing it up, he figured he should double-check that Room 13 really existed.

It wasn't hard for him to decide. There was the door, clearly marked with the number, and he could tell someone was inside—he heard footsteps and what sounded like a voice. As he paused to double-check the number, the footsteps stopped, as if they were right near the door, and he suddenly heard a strange, fast breathing, like someone was very worked up or excited. Feeling a little uneasy, he walked on to his own room. Again, it seemed smaller than it had the night before, which disappointed him slightly—but not too much. If it turned out to be too cramped, he could always switch rooms.

For now, he needed something—he thought it was a handkerchief—from his suitcase. The porter had placed it on a flimsy stool against the far wall, across from the bed. But when he looked, the suitcase was gone. Maybe a well-meaning maid had moved it? He checked the wardrobe, but nothing was there. It was annoying, but he didn't think for a second that it had been stolen—things like that were rare in Denmark. More likely, someone had just been careless, which wasn't uncommon. He decided he'd talk to the maid about it later, but since he didn't need the item right away, he chose not to bother the staff that night.

He went over to the window on the right side of the room and looked out onto the quiet street. Across the way was a tall building with mostly blank walls. There was no one walking by, and the night was dark and still. The lamp behind him cast his shadow on the wall across the street. He could also see the shadow of the man in Room 11, to the left—he walked back and forth in his shirtsleeves, brushing his hair, and later appeared wearing a nightgown.

Then there was the shadow from Room 13, on the right. That one was more interesting. Like Anderson, the figure was leaning on the windowsill, looking out. It seemed tall and thin—possibly a man, though he couldn't be sure. The person had something draped over their head, maybe a scarf or cloth, as if preparing for bed. There was also a flickering red light behind them, probably from a lamp with a red shade. The light danced on the wall in a dull, eerie way.

Anderson leaned out a little more to get a better look, but the only extra detail he could make out was a fold of light-colored cloth lying on the windowsill. Just then, someone's footsteps echoed in the street below, and the figure in Room 13 suddenly pulled back from the window, and the red light went out.

Anderson, finishing his cigarette, stubbed it out on the windowsill and went to bed.

The next morning, the maid came in with hot water. Anderson sat up and, carefully picking his Danish words, said, "You must not move my suitcase. Where is it?"

The maid laughed, which wasn't unusual, and left without answering clearly. Annoyed, Anderson sat up straighter to call her back—but stopped. There was the suitcase, sitting exactly where he remembered the porter putting it on the stool. He stared at it in disbelief. He couldn't explain how he'd missed it the night before. But there it was now.

Morning light revealed more than just the missing suitcase. It showed the true size of the room, with its three windows, and Anderson realized it was actually a good space. Almost fully dressed, he went to the center window to check the weather. Then came another surprise. He had been sure—absolutely sure—that he'd been standing at the right-hand window when he smoked his cigarette before bed. But the stub was on the sill of the middle window.

He shook his head and headed downstairs for breakfast. He was a bit late, but whoever was in Room 13 was even later—their boots were still sitting outside the door. They were clearly a man's boots, so that settled the question of the figure's gender from the night before.

Just then, he glanced at the number on the door. It said 14.

Had he walked past Room 13 without noticing it? That would be odd. Confused, he turned back to double-check. But the room next to 14 was 12—his own.

There was no Room 13 at all.

After spending a few minutes thinking carefully about everything he had eaten and drunk in the past day, Anderson decided to stop trying to figure it out. If his eyes or mind really were starting to fail him, he'd have plenty of time to find out. If not, then something unusual was happening—and either way, it was going to be interesting to see what happened next.

That day, he kept working through the bishop's letters, which we've already talked about. To his disappointment, the collection wasn't complete. Only one more letter mentioned Mag Nicolas Francken. It was written by Bishop Jörgen Friis to Rasmus Nielsen. In it, the Bishop said:

"Even though we strongly disagree with your view of our church court, and are ready to defend it if necessary, the issue no longer matters for now. Our trusted friend, Mag Nicolas Francken, the man you've accused with such false and hateful claims, has suddenly been taken from us. Because of this, there's no more case to discuss. But since you also claim that the Apostle and Evangelist St. John, in his Revelation, described the Holy Roman Church as the Scarlet Woman, let it be known to you..." and so on.

No follow-up letter could be found, and there were no clues about how or why Francken had been "removed." Anderson guessed that he must have died suddenly. Since only two days had passed between Nielsen's last letter—where Francken was still alive—and the Bishop's reply, his death must have come as a complete shock.

That afternoon, Anderson made a short visit to Hald and had tea at Baekkelund. Even though he was still a bit uneasy after the morning's events, he didn't notice any signs that his eyes or mind were playing tricks on him.

At dinner, he found himself sitting next to the landlord. After some casual small talk, Anderson asked, "Why is it that most hotels in this country leave out Room 13? I noticed you don't have one here either."

The landlord smiled, a bit amused. "Funny that you'd pick up on that! I've thought about it myself now and then. I always say, an educated person shouldn't believe in superstitions. I went to the high school here in Viborg, and our old teacher was totally against that kind of thinking. He's been gone for years now—a tall, strong man who didn't just talk, he acted too. I remember us boys one snowy day—"

He drifted into a story from his school days.

"But you don't personally think there's anything wrong with having a Room 13?" Anderson asked when the landlord paused.

"Oh, right, back to that," the landlord said. "Well, I learned the hotel business from my father. He ran a hotel in Aarhus before moving here—this was his hometown—and took over the Phoenix Hotel until he passed in 1876. I opened a place in Silkeborg after that, and only moved into this hotel the year before last."

He went on, talking about the condition the building had been in when he took it over.

"So when you came here, was there a Room 13 already?" Anderson asked.

"No, no. That's just it. In a place like this, most of our guests are business travelers. And those men—put them in Room 13? They'd rather sleep outside! It doesn't matter to me at all what number the room is, and I've told them that plenty of times. But they're convinced it brings bad luck. They've got tons of stories about people who stayed in Room 13 and were never the same, or lost their best customers, or something else went wrong," he said, shrugging and clearly trying to think of a better way to describe it.

"So, what do you use for Room 13 now?" Anderson asked, realizing he felt strangely nervous about the answer.

"My Room 13? Didn't I just say? There's no such room in this house. You probably noticed that. If there were, it would be right next to your room."

"Well, yes, that's what I thought," Anderson said. "It's just... I could have sworn I saw a door marked 13 in that hallway last night. Actually, I think I saw it the night before too."

As expected, Herr Kristensen laughed off the idea and firmly insisted—several times—that Room 13 didn't exist and never had, at least not since he'd taken over the hotel.

Anderson felt somewhat reassured by his certainty, but he was still confused. Maybe the best way to settle the matter, once and for all, was to ask the landlord to come up to his room that evening to smoke a cigar. That would give him an excuse to casually ask again. Luckily, he had some photographs of English towns with him—just the sort of thing to use as a conversation starter.

Herr Kristensen was pleased by the invitation and happily accepted. He said he would come by around ten, but before then, Anderson had some letters to write, so he went to his room to work. He felt a little embarrassed to admit it, even to himself, but he was definitely getting nervous about Room 13. He was so uneasy that, instead of walking past where the door should have been, he went the long way around through the hall by Room 11.

When he got to his room, he quickly looked around. Everything seemed normal—except that strange feeling that the room had somehow gotten smaller again. At least there was no mystery about his luggage tonight. He had unpacked it himself and tucked the empty bag under the bed.

Trying to shake off the weird thoughts about Room 13, he sat down to write. The hallway outside was quiet. Every now and then he heard someone tossing out a pair of boots or a salesman walking past humming. Occasionally, a cart would rattle over the bumpy cobblestone street, or someone would hurry by on the sidewalk.

Anderson finished his letters, ordered some whisky and soda, and went to the window. Across the street was a tall building with blank walls. He watched the shadows it cast.

He remembered that Room 14 had been taken by the lawyer, a quiet man who barely spoke at meals and always read papers while he ate. But apparently, the lawyer liked to let loose when he was alone—because his shadow showed him dancing. Again and again, the thin figure passed across the window, waving its arms and kicking its legs high. It looked like he was barefoot, and the floor must be well built, because not a sound could be heard. It seemed so out of character for the serious lawyer that Anderson began to imagine a whole funny poem about it:

When I return to my hotel
At ten o'clock or so,
The staff all think I'm acting strange—
But I just let that go.

I close my door and take off my shoes,
Then start to spin and slide.
I dance around and never stop,
Even if folks shout from the side.

They bang the walls and raise their voice,
But I don't even try to hide—
I know the rules are on my side.

If the landlord hadn't knocked at that exact moment, Anderson might have written the whole poem. Kristensen seemed a little surprised when he walked in, almost like he, too, noticed something strange about the room—but he didn't say anything. He was very interested in the photographs Anderson had and started telling stories from his life as he looked through them.

The topic of Room 13 hadn't come up yet, and Anderson wasn't sure how to bring it up—until the lawyer next door began to sing. And it wasn't normal singing. It was strange and awful.

The voice was thin, high, and dry, like it hadn't been used in a long time. It would shoot up in pitch and then drop with a long, sad moan, like wind blowing through a chimney or an organ running out of air. It was such a disturbing sound that Anderson felt if he had been alone, he would've run to someone else's room just for company.

Kristensen sat there with his mouth open. "I don't understand it," he said after a moment, wiping sweat off his face. "That's horrible. I heard something like that once before—but I thought it was a cat."

"Is he going crazy?" Anderson asked.

"He must be. What a shame—he's such a good guest. I heard he's doing well in his business and has a young family too."

Just then, there was a knock at the door. Without waiting to be invited in, the lawyer stepped in, looking a mess—his hair was sticking up, and he was clearly angry.

"Excuse me, sir," he said, "but I'd really appreciate it if you would—" He stopped mid-sentence. It was obvious neither Anderson nor Kristensen was responsible for the noise. After a pause, the singing started again, even wilder than before.

"What in the world is going on?" the lawyer cried. "Where is it coming from? Who's doing it? Am I losing my mind?"

"Surely it's coming from your room, Herr Jensen," Anderson said, trying to keep calm. "Maybe there's a cat or something stuck in your chimney?"

It was the best explanation he could think of, but he knew even as he said it that it sounded ridiculous. Still, anything was better than standing there listening to that awful noise and looking at the landlord's pale, sweaty face as he clutched his chair in fear.

"Impossible," said the lawyer. "There's no chimney. I came here because I was sure the noise was coming from this room—it was definitely right next to mine."

"Was there a door between your room and mine?" Anderson asked quickly.

"No," said Herr Jensen, a little sharply. "At least, there wasn't this morning."

"Oh?" said Anderson. "And tonight?"

"I... I'm not sure," the lawyer answered, sounding uncertain.

Just then, the strange singing in the next room stopped. The voice let out a low, creepy laugh, like someone whispering to themselves. The sound made all three men shiver. Then everything went quiet.

"Well?" the lawyer said. "What do you think, Herr Kristensen? What's happening here?"

"I swear, I don't know," said the landlord, clearly scared. "I've never heard anything like that in my life—and I hope I never do again."

"Same here," Jensen said. He muttered something under his breath. Anderson thought it might have been a line from the Psalms in Latin, but he couldn't be sure.

"We need to do something," Anderson said. "Let's all go check the room."

"But that's Herr Jensen's room!" the landlord protested. "He already came out of it!"

"I'm not so sure," Jensen said. "This gentleman might be right. Let's go take a look."

The only things they had that could be used for protection were a walking stick and an umbrella. Nervous but determined, the three men stepped into the hallway. It was quiet, but they could see light coming from under the next door. Anderson and Jensen approached it. Jensen grabbed the handle and gave the door a hard push—but it wouldn't move.

"Herr Kristensen," Jensen said, "go get your strongest worker. We need help to break this door open."

The landlord quickly nodded and hurried away, clearly glad to leave the area. Jensen and Anderson stood in front of the door, staring at it.

"There it is," Anderson said. "Room Number 13."

"Yeah. There's your room, and here's mine," said Jensen.

"My room has three windows in the daylight," Anderson said, trying to laugh, even though he felt nervous.

"Mine too!" said Jensen. He turned to look at Anderson, his back now facing the door.

Right at that moment, the door suddenly opened. A long, bony arm shot out and grabbed at his shoulder. The sleeve was torn and yellow, and the skin was covered in long, gray hairs.

Anderson screamed and pulled Jensen back just in time. The door slammed shut again, and they heard a low, creepy laugh.

Jensen hadn't seen the arm, but when Anderson told him what had happened, he turned pale and panicked. He wanted to run and lock the door behind them.

Before they could leave, the landlord came back with two strong workers. They all looked nervous. Jensen tried to explain what had happened, but his excitement only made the two men more scared.

They dropped their crowbars and said there was no way they were going near that room.

The landlord looked torn—he knew the hotel's reputation was at risk, but he was too scared to go near the door himself.

Then Anderson got an idea.

"So this is the famous Danish courage I've heard about?" he said. "It's not like there's a German behind that door. And even if there were, there are five of us."

That did the trick. Embarrassed, the two servants and Jensen stepped forward toward the door.

"Wait," said Anderson. "Don't rush in. Landlord, stay out here with the lamp. One of you hit the door—but don't go inside when it opens."

They nodded. The younger man stepped up, lifted his crowbar, and hit the top panel of the door as hard as he could.

What happened next shocked everyone.

There was no cracking, no splinters—just a dull thud, like the crowbar had hit solid stone. The man dropped the tool and grabbed his elbow, groaning in pain.

Everyone looked at him. Then Anderson turned back toward the door—only the door was gone.

In its place was a plain plaster wall with a dent where the crowbar had hit.

Room Number 13 had disappeared.

They all stood there, frozen, staring at the empty wall. A rooster crowed in the yard outside. Anderson looked out the hallway window and saw the sky turning pale—it was almost morning.

"Maybe," the landlord said nervously, "you gentlemen would like a different room for tonight? One with two beds?"

Neither Jensen nor Anderson minded sharing a room. After everything that had happened, neither of them felt like sleeping alone. When they each went to their own rooms to grab what they needed for the night, they stuck together—one holding the candle for the other. They both noticed something strange: rooms 12 and 14 each had three windows.

The next morning, they all met again in Room 12. The landlord didn't want to involve anyone from outside, but it was clear something weird was going on and they needed answers. The two hotel workers agreed to help by tearing up part of the floor. They moved the furniture and started pulling up the floorboards near Room 14. It wasn't easy, and they damaged more than a few boards, but eventually they uncovered the space beneath.

You might expect them to find a skeleton—maybe even Mag Nicolas Francken. But no. What they actually discovered was a small copper box lying between the wooden beams. Inside was a folded piece of parchment made of vellum, covered in about twenty lines of writing.

Both Anderson and Jensen—who happened to know a bit about reading old handwriting—were excited. This document might finally explain everything that had happened.

I actually have a book on astrology that I've never really read. The front has an old woodcut illustration by Hans Sebald Beham that shows several wise men sitting at a table. That might help someone recognize the book. I don't remember its name, and it's not near me right now. But I do remember that the inside cover pages are filled with writing. In the ten years I've owned the book, I still haven't figured out which direction the words go—or even what language it's in.

That's kind of how it was for Anderson and Jensen. After studying the paper from the copper box for two full days, they still couldn't make sense of it. Jensen, who was braver, guessed it might be in Latin or Old Danish.

Anderson didn't guess at all. He just handed the box and parchment over to the Historical Society of Viborg so they could put it in their museum.

He told me this entire story a few months later, while we were sitting in the woods near Uppsala. We had just come from the library, where we found a strange old document. It was a contract written by Daniel Salthenius—who later became a Hebrew professor in Königsberg—when he was still a student. In it, he promised his soul to the devil. I laughed when I read it, but Anderson didn't.

"Foolish kid," he said, shaking his head. "Did he even know what kind of thing he was inviting?"

I tried to joke, but Anderson just grunted. Later that day, he told me the story you've just read. But even then, he wouldn't say what he thought it meant—and he didn't agree with any of the ideas I had, either.

Count Magnus

The way I came to have the papers this story is based on is something I'll explain at the very end. But before I share what's in them, I need to describe the form they were in when I found them.

They're partly made up of notes and drafts for a travel book, the kind that was popular in the 1840s and 1850s. Books like Journal of a Residence in Jutland and the Danish Isles by Horace Marryat are good examples. These kinds of books usually described places in Europe that weren't very well known. They often included woodcut or steel illustrations, tips on where to stay, how to get around, and stories of chats with locals—whether clever, funny, or just chatty.

What started out as material for a travel book slowly turned into a personal journal. It became a record of one man's strange experience, written up until just before it came to an end.

The author was a man named Mr. Wraxall. Everything I know about him comes from his own writing. From what I've read, he was probably middle-aged or older, had some money of his own, and lived alone. He didn't have a permanent home in England—he stayed in hotels and boarding houses. It seems like he meant to settle down at some point, but never did. He also mentioned a few times that some of his belongings were stored at the Pantechnicon, which burned down in the early 1870s. That fire may have destroyed other records of his life.

Mr. Wraxall had written at least one book, based on a trip he took to Brittany. I don't know the title of the book or what name he used, because I couldn't find it in any catalog. He may have published it anonymously or under a fake name.

As for what kind of person he was—it's not too hard to get a sense of him. He was smart, well-educated, and curious. According to the Oxford calendar, he almost became a Fellow at Brasenose College. But he may have been too curious for his own good. That kind of curiosity can be useful when you're a traveler, but for Mr. Wraxall, it ended up costing him dearly.

On what turned out to be his last trip, he was planning another book. At the time, Scandinavia was still unfamiliar to most English readers, and he saw an opportunity to write something new. He had come across some old Swedish history books or memoirs, and got the idea to write about traveling in Sweden, mixed with stories about old noble families. He got letters of introduction to help him meet the right people and set off in early summer of 1863.

There's no need to go into detail about his travels in Sweden or his stay in Stockholm. What matters is that, while there, a local scholar pointed him toward a collection of family documents owned by the people living in an old manor in the region of Västergötland. The scholar also helped him get permission to go there and read through the papers.

The manor—called a herrgård in Swedish—will be referred to here as Råbäck (pronounced kind of like "Roebeck"), though that's not its real name. It's one of the finest manor houses in the country, and a 1694 engraving in Suecia antiqua et moderna by Dahlenberg shows it looking pretty much the same as it does today. It was built shortly after 1600 and resembles an English house from that time—made of red brick with stone edges and similar in style.

The original builder was a member of the powerful De la Gardie family, and his descendants still own the house. I'll refer to the family as the De la Gardies whenever I need to mention them.

Mr. Wraxall was welcomed warmly and kindly by the family at the manor. They invited him to stay in the house for as long as he needed to finish his research. But he preferred to stay on his own and wasn't confident in his Swedish, so he chose to stay at the village inn instead. It was actually quite comfortable, at least during the summer. Staying there meant he'd have to walk less than a mile to the manor-house every day.

The manor sat in a large park filled with tall, old trees. Close by, there was a walled garden, and just beyond that, a thick forest that bordered one of the many small lakes scattered across the area. After the woods came a stone wall marking the edge of the estate. Past the wall, a rocky hill covered in a thin layer of soil rose steeply, and at the top stood the local church. Tall, dark trees surrounded it.

To someone from England, the church looked unusual. The main section and side aisles were low, filled with rows of pews and small balconies. A grand old organ stood in the balcony at the back, brightly painted and decorated with silver pipes. The ceiling was flat and had a dramatic and eerie painting of the Last Judgment, filled with fire, falling cities, burning ships, screaming souls, and demons with smiling brown faces. Fancy brass chandeliers hung from the ceiling. The pulpit looked like a toy house, covered in tiny painted angels and saints. On the preacher's stand was a rack holding three hourglasses to time the sermons. While many Swedish churches have things like this, one part of this church made it unique.

At the far end of the north aisle, the original owner of the manor had built a special burial room—a mausoleum—for himself and his family. It was an eight-sided structure with oval windows and a domed roof topped with a spire shaped like a pumpkin, a style popular with Swedish architects. The outside roof was made of copper and painted black, while the walls, like those of the church, were bright white. This building wasn't connected to the church from the inside; it had its own entrance and steps on the north side.

The village path passed by the churchyard, and from there, it only took a few minutes to reach the inn.

On his first day in Råbäck, Mr. Wraxall found the church door open and made notes on everything inside, as I've just described. But he couldn't get into the mausoleum. Peeking through the keyhole, he could just make out marble statues, copper coffins, and lots of decorative symbols. He really wanted a closer look.

The documents he came to study at the manor were exactly what he needed for his book. They included family letters, journals, and financial records from the estate's earliest owners. Everything was clearly written and full of vivid, interesting details. The first De la Gardie was described as a strong and determined man. Not long after he built the mansion, a local crisis led to a peasant uprising. Several nearby estates were attacked. The owner of Råbäck helped put down the rebellion and punished the ringleaders harshly.

Mr. Wraxall found a portrait of this man—Count Magnus de la Gardie—hanging in the manor and studied it closely. He didn't describe it in great detail, but wrote that the Count didn't look kind or attractive—he looked powerful, even frightening. In fact, he said Count Magnus was almost shockingly ugly.

That evening, Mr. Wraxall had supper with the family and walked back to the inn under the still-bright evening sky.

"I must remember," he wrote in his notes, "to ask the church sexton if he can let me into the mausoleum. He clearly has the key, because I saw him standing there tonight, either locking or unlocking the door."

The next morning, Mr. Wraxall spoke with his innkeeper. At first, it seemed odd that he wrote down the whole conversation. But it soon became clear that these notes were meant for his travel book, which would include bits of dialogue and local color.

Wraxall wanted to know if the local people still remembered Count Magnus, and if they thought of him in a good or bad light. It turned out the Count wasn't remembered fondly. If his workers showed up late on days they owed him, they were punished—forced to sit on a wooden horse, whipped, or even branded in the manor yard. In a few cases, people who lived on land that overlapped the Count's were said to have died in fires that destroyed their homes in the middle of winter, with their entire families inside.

But what the innkeeper kept bringing up, more than anything else, was something even stranger: the Count had taken the "Black Pilgrimage" and returned with something—or someone.

You're probably wondering, just like Mr. Wraxall did, what the Black Pilgrimage was. But for now, your curiosity—like his—will have to wait. The innkeeper clearly didn't want to talk about it. He avoided answering completely, and when he was called away to do something in the town of Skara, he left in a hurry. A few minutes later, he stuck his head back in the room just to say he wouldn't be back until that evening.

So, without answers, Mr. Wraxall went off to continue his work at the manor-house. The documents he was reading soon distracted him, since they were letters between Sophia Albertina in Stockholm and her cousin Ulrica Leonora, who lived at Råbäck, during the years 1705 to 1710. These letters gave an interesting look at life and culture in Sweden during that time—something you can see for yourself if you've read the full edition printed by the Swedish Historical Manuscripts Commission.

That afternoon, once he'd finished reading those letters and returned the boxes to their place on the shelf, he started looking at the other books nearby to choose what to read next. Most of the books on that shelf were account books, written by the first Count Magnus. But one of them stood out. It wasn't about finances—it was full of strange texts on alchemy and other unusual topics, written in a handwriting from the 1500s.

Wraxall wasn't very familiar with alchemy, so he spent quite a bit of time listing the titles and introductions of the treatises inside: The Book of the Phoenix, Book of the Thirty Words, Book of the Toad, Book of Miriam, Turba Philosophorum, and others. But what really grabbed his attention was a short note written on a blank page in the middle of the book. It was in Count Magnus's own handwriting, and the title at the top said Liber nigræ peregrinationis—which means Book of the Black Pilgrimage.

There were only a few lines of writing, but enough to show that what the landlord had mentioned earlier wasn't just a rumor—it was based on a belief that went back to Count Magnus's time, and possibly came from the Count himself. This is what the English translation said:

"If any man wishes to live a long life, to gain a loyal servant, and to see the blood of his enemies, he must first travel to the city of Chorazin and greet the prince…"

There was a word that had been scratched out, but not very well. Wraxall was pretty sure it said aëris—Latin for "of the air." After that, the note ended with one last Latin line: Quære reliqua hujus materiei inter secretiora—which means, "Look for the rest of this subject among the secret writings."

It was clear from this that Count Magnus had some very dark interests. But Wraxall, who lived three centuries later, didn't find it disturbing—he thought it made the Count even more fascinating. The idea that someone so powerful had also studied alchemy, or even magic, added mystery to his image. That evening, after spending some time staring at the Count's portrait in the manor hall, Wraxall walked back toward the inn. His thoughts were so full of Count Magnus that he hardly noticed the woods, the scent of the trees, or the soft light on the lake. He only snapped out of it when he found himself already standing at the churchyard gate, just a few minutes away from dinner.

He looked toward the family tomb and said aloud, "Ah, Count Magnus, there you are. I'd really love to see you."

He added later in his notes, "Like a lot of people who spend time alone, I talk to myself out loud sometimes. But unlike in Greek or Latin grammar, I don't expect a reply."

Luckily—maybe—it seemed no one was around to answer. The only sound was a woman inside the church dropping something metallic, which startled him.

"I think Count Magnus is sleeping soundly," he wrote.

Later that same evening, the innkeeper, who had heard Wraxall say he wanted to meet the church clerk (or deacon, as he would be called in Sweden), introduced them in the inn's sitting room. They quickly made plans to visit the De la Gardie tomb the next day, and then chatted about other things.

Wraxall, knowing that deacons in Sweden often help teach people preparing for confirmation, decided to ask a Bible-related question to refresh his memory.

"Can you tell me anything about Chorazin?" he asked.

The deacon looked surprised but answered right away. He reminded Wraxall that Chorazin had once been cursed in the Bible.

"Right," said Wraxall. "It's just a ruin now, isn't it?"

"I think so," the deacon replied. "I've heard some of the older priests say that Antichrist is supposed to be born there. And there are stories—"

"What kind of stories?" Mr. Wraxall asked quickly.

"Well," said the deacon, "stories I've forgotten." And soon after that, he said good night and left.

Now the landlord was alone with Mr. Wraxall, who wasn't about to let the chance go. He was ready with questions.

"Herr Nielsen," Wraxall said, "I've learned a little about the Black Pilgrimage. You might as well tell me what you know. What exactly did the Count bring back with him?"

Swedes often take their time to respond, or maybe this landlord was just an exception. Either way, Mr. Wraxall noted that the man stared at him silently for nearly a full minute before finally stepping closer and speaking, clearly with some effort:

"Mr. Wraxall, I'll tell you one short story. Just one. You must promise not to ask more when I'm done.

"This happened in my grandfather's time—ninety-two years ago. There were two men who said, 'The Count is dead. We don't care about him anymore. Tonight, we're going to hunt in his woods for free.' They meant the big woods on the hill behind Råbäck that you've seen.

"People who heard them warned them not to go. They said, 'Don't do it. We believe there are people walking in those woods who shouldn't be. They should be resting, not wandering around.'

"But the two men just laughed. There were no guards in the forest because nobody wanted to live out there, and the Count's family wasn't staying at the house. So they thought they could do whatever they liked.

"Well, that night, my grandfather was sitting right here in this room. It was summer, and the nights were light. He had the window open and could see the woods in the distance.

"He and two or three others sat there, listening. At first, it was quiet. Then, far off, they heard a scream—a terrible scream, like someone's soul was being ripped from their body. Everyone in the room grabbed each other, frozen in fear. They sat that way for about 45 minutes.

"Then they heard something else—another sound, much closer now, only a few hundred yards away. This time it was laughter—but not from one of the two men. No, everyone agreed it didn't sound like a human laugh at all. After that, they heard a huge door slam shut.

"When the sky started to lighten with the sunrise, they all went to the priest.

"'Father,' they said, 'put on your robe and your white collar. You need to come and bury these two men—Anders Bjornsen and Hans Thorbjorn.'

"They were sure both men were dead. So the priest and the others walked out to the forest. My grandfather never forgot what he saw that day. He said they all looked like ghosts themselves, pale and shaken. Even the priest was terrified. He told them, 'I heard someone scream last night, and then I heard someone laugh. If I can't forget those sounds, I won't sleep again.'

"They found the men at the edge of the woods. Hans Thorbjorn was standing upright with his back against a tree. He kept pushing at something with his hands—something that wasn't there. He was alive, but clearly not okay. They took him to the hospital in Nyköping, where he died before winter. Even until the end, he kept pushing the air with his hands.

"Anders Bjornsen was also there. But he was dead. I'll tell you this—he used to be a very handsome man, but now his face was gone. The flesh had been sucked off his skull. Do you understand? My grandfather said he could never forget that.

"They put his body on a stretcher and covered his face with a cloth. The priest walked ahead, and they began to sing the funeral hymn as best they could. But as they finished the first verse, one of the men at the front of the stretcher collapsed. The others turned to look—and saw that the cloth had slipped off. Anders's eyes were wide open and staring, because there were no eyelids left to close them.

"No one could stand the sight of it. So the priest quickly put the cloth back over his face, called for a shovel, and they buried him right there on the spot."

The next day, Mr. Wraxall wrote that the deacon came to get him shortly after breakfast and took him to the church and the mausoleum. He noticed that the key to the tomb was hanging on a nail near the pulpit. Since the church door usually stayed unlocked, he realized it wouldn't be hard to come back later on his own if the monuments inside turned out to be more interesting than he could fully appreciate during this first visit.

Once inside, he found the building impressive. Most of the tombs were large, built in the 1600s and 1700s, and decorated with lots of writing and family symbols. In the middle of the domed room stood three copper coffins, each covered with detailed designs. Two of them had large metal crosses on top, which was common in Sweden and Denmark. The third one, which seemed to belong to Count Magnus, was different. Instead of a cross, it had a full-body engraving of the Count, and the edges were decorated with scenes.

One picture showed a battle with cannons, smoke, walled cities, and soldiers with spears. Another showed an execution. In a third, a man was running through trees, his hair flying and arms stretched out. He was being chased by something strange. It wasn't clear if the artist had meant to draw a person but failed, or if it was supposed to be a monster. Given how detailed the rest of the drawings were, Wraxall thought the creature was meant to look scary. It was short, wore a long hooded cloak that dragged on the ground, and the only part of it sticking out didn't look like a normal hand or arm. Wraxall said it reminded him of an octopus tentacle.

He thought, "This must be some kind of symbol—like a demon chasing a soul. Maybe that's where the story of Count Magnus and his mysterious follower came from." Curious, he looked for the hunter in the picture, expecting to see a demon with a horn. But all he saw was a cloaked man standing on a hill, leaning on a walking stick, watching everything calmly.

Wraxall also noticed three large steel padlocks on the Count's coffin. One of them had fallen off and was lying on the floor. Not wanting to keep the deacon waiting or lose more time from his research, he left for the manor house.

"It's strange," he wrote later, "how when you walk a path you know well, your thoughts can distract you so much that you forget where you are. That evening, for the second time, I found myself at the churchyard gate without meaning to be there. I think I was singing to myself—something like, 'Are you awake, Count Magnus? Are you asleep, Count Magnus?' and maybe something else I can't remember. It was like I had been walking and talking nonsense without realizing it."

He found the mausoleum key just where he expected and copied most of the information he wanted. He stayed until the daylight faded.

"I must have been wrong when I said one of the coffin's locks was open," he wrote later. "Tonight, I saw that two of them were unfastened. I picked them up and placed them on the window ledge, but I couldn't get them to snap shut. The last lock is still tightly closed. I think it's a spring lock, but I have no idea how it opens. Honestly, if I'd figured it out, I think I might have opened the coffin—I'm not sure that would've been wise. But I can't help how interested I am in this rather scary and fierce old nobleman."

The following day turned out to be Mr. Wraxall's last at Råbäck. He got some letters about his finances that made it necessary for him to return to England. His research was nearly finished anyway, and travel would take time. So he decided to say his goodbyes, finish his notes, and start heading home.

Finishing his goodbyes and wrapping up his work ended up taking Mr. Wraxall more time than expected. The family at the manor warmly invited him to stay for dinner—they ate at three in the afternoon—and it was nearly 6:30 by the time he stepped outside the iron gates of Råbäck. Wanting to fully take in the atmosphere one last time, he walked slowly by the lake, soaking in every detail of the view and the feeling of the place. When he reached the hilltop near the churchyard, he paused for a while, gazing out over the dark woods stretching across the land under a soft green sky.

As he turned to leave, a thought struck him—shouldn't he say goodbye to Count Magnus too, just like he had to the rest of the De la Gardie family? The church was only a short distance away, and he knew where the key to the tomb was kept. Before long, he found himself once again standing over the Count's large copper coffin, talking out loud to himself as usual. "Maybe you weren't the nicest person, Magnus," he said, "but still, I'd kind of like to see you. Or maybe—"

Just then, something hit his foot. He quickly stepped back, and something clattered to the floor. It was the third and final padlock from the sarcophagus. He bent down to pick it up—and he swore to himself he was telling the honest truth—but before he could stand back up, he heard metal hinges creak and saw the lid of the coffin beginning to lift.

Maybe he acted like a coward, he wrote, but there was no way he could stay. He ran out of that terrible place faster than he could write or even say it out loud. What scared him even more was that once he got outside, he couldn't get the key to turn and lock the door. As he sat in his room writing down what had happened—not even twenty minutes later—he couldn't remember if that creaking noise had continued or not. But he knew something else had scared him even more than what he wrote—though whether it was something he heard or saw, he couldn't say.

"What have I done?" he asked himself.

Poor Mr. Wraxall. He left for England the very next day, just as he had planned, and he arrived safely. But based on the way his handwriting changed and how scattered his notes became, it's clear something had shaken him badly. One of the small notebooks that came with his other papers gives a glimpse into what happened next.

He traveled much of the way home by canal-boat and tried several times to list and describe the people on board. Each time, he recorded 28 passengers, including a man in a long black cloak and wide-brimmed hat, and a shorter figure in a dark hooded cloak. But at meals, there were only ever 26 people. The man in the cloak might be missing, but the hooded figure was always absent.

After arriving in England, Mr. Wraxall landed in Harwich. He seemed sure that someone—or something—was following him. Without trusting the trains, he hired a closed carriage and traveled across the countryside to a small village called Belchamp St. Paul. It was around 9 p.m. on a moonlit night when he got close. He was sitting forward, staring out the window as fields and trees sped by.

Suddenly, at a crossroads, he saw two still figures standing by the road. Both wore dark cloaks—one tall with a hat, the other shorter with a hood. He couldn't see their faces, and they didn't move. But his horse reared back in fright and then bolted forward. Wraxall dropped back into his seat in terror. He had seen those two before.

When he arrived in the village, he found a quiet, furnished place to stay. For the next day or so, things seemed calm. He even wrote a few last notes. But those final writings were scattered and frantic. It's clear he was waiting for a visit—he didn't know when or how it would happen, but he believed it was coming. He kept asking, "What did I do?" and "Is there any hope?" He felt sure that doctors would just think he was insane and police wouldn't believe him. The local priest was away. In the end, all he could do was lock his door and pray.

People in the village still remember the story. Years ago, a strange man showed up one evening in August. The morning after next, he was found dead. There was an inquest, but it was odd—seven jurors fainted when they saw the body, and none would say what they saw. The official verdict was "visitation of God." The family who owned the house moved out within a week and never came back to the area.

No one ever found out what really happened—or if it could even be explained.

As it turns out, I inherited that very house last year as part of a will. It had stood empty since 1863, and there was no chance of renting it out, so I had it torn down. That's when we found the papers I've just shared with you, hidden in a forgotten cupboard beneath the window of the best bedroom.

"Oh, Whistle, And I'll Come To You, My Lad"

"I guess you'll be heading out soon now that Full Term is over, Professor," said someone who isn't part of this story, talking to the Professor of Ontography as they sat down together at a formal dinner at St. James's College.

The Professor was a young man—tidy, well-spoken, and very precise.

"Yes," he said. "Some friends convinced me to take up golf this term, so I'm planning to go to the East Coast—actually to Burnstow, if you know it—for about a week or ten days to practice. I hope to leave tomorrow."

"Oh, Parkins," said the person sitting on his other side, "since you're going to Burnstow, could you check out the site of the Templars' old preceptory while you're there? Let me know if you think it would be worth digging into this summer."

This second man was clearly interested in historical research, but since he only shows up briefly, we don't need to name him.

"Of course," said Parkins. "If you describe where the site is, I'll do my best to check it out and tell you what the land looks like. Or I can write to you if you tell me where you'll be staying."

"No need to write, thanks. I'm just thinking of taking my family out that way over the summer. Not many old Templar sites have been properly studied, and I might have some time to work on it in between family stuff."

The Professor didn't seem to think much of that kind of project being called "useful," but he didn't say anything. The other man went on:

"The site—I doubt there's anything visible left—is probably right near the beach now. The sea's eaten away a lot of the coast in that area. From the map, I'd guess it's about three-quarters of a mile from the Globe Inn, on the north side of town. Where are you staying?"

"At the Globe Inn, actually," said Parkins. "I've booked a room there. It was the only place available—most of the lodgings close for the winter, apparently. Even there, the only room big enough is a double room, and they say they don't have anywhere to store the extra bed. Still, I needed a good-sized room since I'm bringing books and plan to do a bit of writing. I'm not thrilled about having an extra bed— or two—in what's going to be my study, but I guess I can deal with it for a short trip."

"You call that roughing it?" said a loud man across the table. "Tell you what, I'll come down and take that extra bed for a bit. Keep you company."

Parkins looked uncomfortable but managed to laugh politely.

"Sure, Rogers, I'd like that. But I'm worried you might get bored— I don't think you play golf, do you?"

"No, thank goodness," said the blunt Mr. Rogers.

"Well, you see, when I'm not writing, I'll probably be out on the golf course. That might not be much fun for you."

"Oh, I'm sure I'll find someone I know there. But seriously, if you don't want me to come, just say so—I won't take it personally. As you always say, the truth isn't rude."

Parkins was always polite and honest, which Rogers liked to tease him about. Right now, Parkins was stuck in an awkward moment, unsure what to say. After a short pause, he finally answered:

"If you want the honest truth, Rogers, I was just wondering if the room would actually be big enough for both of us. And also—(and I wouldn't have said this if you hadn't pushed me)—I'm afraid you might end up being a distraction from my work."

Rogers laughed loudly.

"Well said, Parkins!" he said. "Don't worry—I won't mess with your work. I won't come if you don't want me. I just thought I might be good to have around in case you need someone to scare off the ghosts." He winked and nudged the person next to him. Parkins blushed.

"Sorry, Parkins," Rogers added. "I shouldn't have said that. I forgot you don't like jokes about that kind of thing."

"Well," Parkins said, "since you brought it up, I'll be honest—I don't like it when people joke about ghosts. In my line of work," he added, raising his voice a little, "I have to be very careful not to make it seem like I believe in that sort of thing. You know that, Rogers—or at least you should. I've never kept my views a secret—"

"No, you definitely haven't," Rogers muttered quietly.

"—I believe that even hinting these things might be real goes against everything I believe in. But I can see I haven't exactly kept your full attention."

"'Your undivided attention,' is what Dr. Blimber actually said," Rogers interrupted, pretending to be helpful. "But sorry, Parkins, go ahead."

"It's fine," Parkins replied. "I don't remember Dr. Blimber—maybe he was before my time. But anyway, I think you get what I mean."

"Yes, yes," said Rogers quickly. "We can talk more about it at Burnstow or something."

From this conversation, it's easy to see that Parkins was a bit fussy and old-fashioned. He didn't really have a sense of humor, but he was brave and truly believed in what he stood for. Whether or not the reader feels the same, that's the kind of man he was.

The next day, just like he'd planned, Parkins left his college and arrived in Burnstow. The Globe Inn welcomed him, and he got settled into the large room with two beds that had been mentioned earlier. Before going to bed, he carefully arranged his books and papers on a large table at the far end of the room. The table was surrounded by three windows, all facing the sea. The middle window looked straight out at the water. The left one showed the coastline stretching north, and the right one looked toward the village to the south. There were no buildings to the north—just the beach and a low cliff. Right in front of the inn was a small patch of rough grass with old anchors and other gear lying around, then a wide path, and then the beach itself. The sea was now only about sixty yards from the inn.

Most of the other guests at the inn were golfers, and there wasn't much about them that stood out. One man, though, was hard to miss. He was a retired military officer and a club secretary from London. He had a booming voice and strong opinions—especially when it came to religion. After attending church, he often shared his views loudly. The local vicar, who preferred a more traditional and decorative church service, tried to keep things plain to match the East Anglian style.

Parkins, who was known for being brave, spent most of the day after his arrival working on his golf skills with this same Colonel Wilson.

By the afternoon, whether because of the golf or something else, the Colonel was in such a bad mood that Parkins decided it would be best not to walk back with him. After sneaking a glance at his red face and bristly mustache, Parkins figured it was smarter to let the Colonel cool off with some tea and a smoke before dinner.

"Maybe I'll walk home along the beach tonight," Parkins thought. "And I'll try to find those ruins Disney mentioned. There should still be enough light. I don't know exactly where they are, but I'll probably come across them sooner or later."

Parkins managed to find the ruins, though not exactly on purpose. While making his way from the golf course to the rocky beach, he tripped—partly on a gorse root and partly on a large stone—and fell over. When he stood up and looked around, he realized he was standing in a rough area of land filled with small dips and grassy mounds. After looking more closely, he saw the mounds were just clumps of flint rocks held together with old mortar, covered over with grass. He figured, correctly, that this must be the spot where the old Templars' preceptory once stood.

He thought it might be a great site for an archaeological dig. There were probably still enough of the building's foundations under the surface to help map out the layout. He remembered that the Templars often built round churches, and he noticed that some of the mounds seemed to form a rough circle. Like many people, Parkins couldn't resist trying a bit of amateur archaeology, partly for the fun of it and partly because he genuinely wanted to help his friend Mr. Disney.

So, he carefully walked around the circular area and jotted down rough measurements in his notebook. Then he checked out a long raised section on the east side of the circle, which he thought might have been the base of an altar or platform. At one end—the north side—some of the grass had been pulled away, probably by a curious kid or an animal. Parkins thought it wouldn't hurt to dig a little and see if there were any signs of a stone structure underneath. He pulled out his pocketknife and started gently scraping away the soil.

Soon, a bit of the earth gave way, revealing a small hole. He tried to light a few matches to get a better look, but the wind kept blowing them out. Still, by tapping and feeling with his knife, he realized the hole wasn't natural—it had been made by someone. It was a small, rectangular space with smooth walls, like it had been plastered or carefully built. He figured it would be empty.

But no—it wasn't.

When he reached in with his hand, he heard a soft metal clink. He felt around and pulled out a small, metal cylinder about four inches long. It was clearly man-made and looked quite old. Parkins checked to make sure there was nothing else inside the little hole. By then, the sun was going down, and it was too dark to continue exploring. But what he'd found was interesting enough that he decided to come back the next day and dig a little more.

He slipped the object into his pocket and looked around one last time before heading back. The view was cold and lonely. The fading yellow light in the west lit up the golf course, where a few people were still walking back to the clubhouse. He could see the squat Martello tower, the lights of Aldsey village, the pale line of the beach, the dark wooden sea defenses, and the quiet waves. The wind was icy and blew from the north, but at least it was pushing him forward on his walk to the inn.

He crunched over the loose stones, then reached the sand, which was much easier to walk on—except for the wooden barriers spaced every few yards. Just before moving on, he glanced behind him to see how far he'd come since leaving the ruined church. That's when he noticed someone following him.

It was a blurry figure, moving like they were trying to catch up—but not actually getting any closer. Parkins thought it looked like the person was running, but the space between them never seemed to change. He figured he didn't know the person and thought it would be silly to stop and wait.

Still, a little company would've been nice on that empty beach—if only he could choose who it was. His mind drifted to creepy stories he'd read as a kid, stories about people meeting strange beings in places just like this. He couldn't stop thinking about one in particular, a favorite from childhood: "Now I saw in my dream that Christian had gone but a very little way when he saw a foul fiend coming over the field to meet him."

"What would I do," Parkins wondered, "if I looked back and saw a black figure against the yellow sky with horns and wings? Would I run or stand still?" Then he reassured himself. "Luckily, whoever's behind me isn't anything like that—and they're still just as far away as when I first saw them."

He chuckled to himself. "At this rate, he's going to miss dinner, and I'll get mine first. And speaking of which—oh no, it's almost dinner time already. I'd better run!"

Parkins didn't have much time to get ready for dinner. When he finally sat down with Colonel Wilson, the Colonel seemed to be in a much better mood—or as calm as he could be. Things stayed peaceful even during the card games after dinner, thanks in part to Parkins being a pretty decent player. By the time he headed up to his room around midnight, he felt satisfied with how the evening had gone. He thought to himself that even if he had to stay at the Globe Inn for two or three weeks, it wouldn't be so bad—especially if his golf game kept improving.

As he walked through the hallway, the hotel's boot boy stopped him and said, "Excuse me, sir. While I was brushing your coat, something fell out of the pocket. I left it on your dresser. Looked like part of a pipe or something, sir. Good night!"

That reminder made Parkins think of what he'd found earlier that day. Curious, he picked it up and looked at it under the candlelight. It was bronze and shaped a lot like a modern dog whistle. Actually, yes—it really was a whistle. He put it to his lips to try it, but it was filled with packed dirt that wouldn't come out just by tapping it. He'd need to scrape it clean.

Being as neat as ever, Parkins used his knife to dig out the dirt and collected it on a piece of paper. Then he walked to the window, opened it, and dumped the dirt outside. The night was clear and bright, and while standing there, he noticed someone out on the shore. The person wasn't moving, just standing there in front of the inn. That struck him as a little odd for the hour. Still, he closed the window, a bit surprised people in Burnstow stayed out so late.

Back under the light, Parkins took another look at the whistle. Wait—were those letters on it? Yes, after rubbing it a bit, he could see the markings clearly. They were deeply carved into the metal, but even after thinking it over, he couldn't figure out what they meant. His Latin was a bit rusty, he admitted to himself.

There were two short lines of writing. One read: FLA FUR BIS FLE

The other: QUIS EST ISTE QUI VENIT

"I should know this," he thought. "The second part's easy enough—it probably means 'Who is this who is coming?' The best way to find out, I guess, is to blow the whistle."

He gave it a light blow—and stopped right away, surprised and a little impressed by the sound. It was soft but carried a strange, faraway tone, as if the sound could travel for miles. Something about it made pictures pop into his mind—like how some smells can bring back memories. For a moment, he clearly imagined a wide, dark landscape at night, with a strong wind blowing and a lone figure standing in the middle. He couldn't tell what the person was doing. The vision faded suddenly when a gust of wind hit his window, just in time for him to spot the flash of a seabird's wing outside.

That eerie sound stuck with him, and he couldn't help but try the whistle again—this time with a bit more confidence. The sound wasn't any louder, and it didn't bring another mental image like before. Still, the wind outside had grown stronger. "Wow," he thought, "I can't believe how quickly it's picked up. What a gust! I knew that window latch was no good. Of course—there go the candles."

Both flames blew out, and the wind rattled everything in the room. Parkins rushed to the window and pushed it closed—it was like trying to shove back a strong man. For a few seconds, it felt like the wind was physically fighting him. Then it suddenly eased up, and the window slammed shut and latched itself.

Next, he re-lit the candles to check for damage, but everything seemed fine. Nothing had broken—not even the glass in the window. But someone else in the building had clearly been woken up. He could hear the Colonel pacing upstairs in his socks, grumbling as he went.

The stormy wind didn't die down right away. It howled and moaned outside, sometimes rising into a sound so lonely and intense that, as Parkins thought, it might make more sensitive people really uneasy. Even someone with a steady mind, he figured after about fifteen minutes, might wish it would stop.

Whether it was the wind, the golf, or the excitement of finding the whistle, Parkins couldn't fall asleep. He lay awake, imagining all sorts of terrible health problems—like many of us do late at night. He counted his heartbeats, worrying they might suddenly stop. He convinced himself something was wrong with his lungs, or his brain, or his liver. Of course, he was sure all those fears would disappear with the morning light, but until then, they felt very real.

He found some strange comfort in knowing he wasn't the only one having trouble sleeping. From nearby—though it was too dark to tell exactly where—he heard someone else tossing and turning in their bed too.

Parkins closed his eyes, determined to finally get some sleep. But instead of drifting off, his mind started playing tricks on him—it created vivid pictures, which happens sometimes when people try too hard to fall asleep. The images were so disturbing that he had to keep opening his eyes to make them stop. Yet every time he closed them again, the same scene returned, exactly as before, playing out from beginning to end without speeding up or slowing down.

What he saw looked just like the beach he'd walked along that afternoon: pebbles and sand, with wooden groynes stretching into the sea. The sky was dark, like a winter evening before a storm, with a light rain falling. At first, there was no one around. Then, far off in the distance, something small and dark began to move. It turned out to be a man, running, jumping over the groynes, and constantly glancing behind him. As he got closer, it was clear he was terrified and completely exhausted. He struggled more with each groyne, and

Parkins found himself thinking, "Can he make it over this one? It looks taller than the others."

Barely, the man did. He half-climbed, half-threw himself over it and collapsed on the other side, crouching low and clearly too tired to get up. He looked around fearfully, hiding.

So far, nothing explained what the man was running from. But then, way up the beach, something pale started flickering back and forth at a crazy speed. It got bigger as it came closer and looked like a person in loose, fluttering clothes. The way it moved made Parkins not want to see it up close. It would pause, lift its arms, bow toward the sand, then dart toward the water and back again, only to straighten up and keep racing forward—faster and more eerily each time.

Soon it was just beyond the groyne, only a few feet from where the man was hiding. It swayed left and right, searching. Then it stopped, stood straight with arms raised, and suddenly rushed right toward the groyne.

That was always the moment when Parkins had to open his eyes. He couldn't take it anymore. Worried that something might be wrong with his eyes or brain—or that maybe he'd smoked too much—he gave up trying to sleep. Instead, he decided to light a candle and read, thinking it was better to stay awake than to keep seeing that creepy vision.

As he struck the match, the sudden light scared something in the room—probably a rat or some other night creature—which he heard scurry across the floor by his bed. Unfortunately, the first match went out too fast. But the second worked better, and he managed to light the candle and find a book.

He read for a while, and soon, real sleep finally came—peaceful and deep. For the first time in his normally careful and tidy life, Parkins forgot to blow out the candle before bed. When the maid came to wake him at 8 a.m., the candle was still barely burning, and wax had melted all over the little table.

After breakfast, Parkins was back in his room getting ready for golf—he was paired again with the Colonel—when one of the maids came in.

"Excuse me, sir," she said, "would you like an extra blanket on your bed?"

"Yes, thank you," said Parkins. "It's probably going to get colder."

The maid returned quickly with the blanket. "Which bed should I put it on, sir?" she asked.

"What? That one," said Parkins, pointing. "The one I slept in."

"Oh! I'm sorry, sir, it's just—you seemed to have used both beds. We had to make them both this morning."

"Really? That's strange," said Parkins. "I didn't touch the other bed, except maybe to place a few things on it. Did it really look like someone slept in it?"

"Oh yes, sir," said the maid. "The sheets were all rumpled and tossed around, if you don't mind me saying—like someone had a very rough night."

"Huh," said Parkins. "Well, maybe I messed it up more than I realized when I unpacked. I'm sorry you had to fix it. Actually, I'm expecting a friend from Cambridge to visit soon. He might use that bed for a night or two. That's all right, isn't it?"

"Oh yes, of course, sir. No trouble at all," the maid replied before leaving—most likely to go laugh about it with the other staff.

Parkins set out with a strong goal in mind: to get better at golf.

I'm happy to report that he made good progress—so much that the Colonel, who hadn't been thrilled about playing another round with him, started to warm up. As the morning went on, he even became quite talkative, his loud voice booming across the open field, much like the deep bell of a church tower.

"That wind last night was something else," the Colonel said. "Back where I'm from, we'd say someone had been whistling for it."

"Really?" Parkins replied. "Do people still believe in things like that where you live?"

"I don't know if it's belief or superstition," said the Colonel. "But folks in Denmark, Norway, and even along the Yorkshire coast think it's true. And I've learned that there's often something behind these old country stories. People don't hang on to them for generations without a reason. But it's your turn now."

Later, when they were chatting again, Parkins said a little hesitantly, "Speaking of what you mentioned earlier, Colonel, I should probably tell you I have strong views on those topics. I don't believe in anything 'supernatural.'"

"You don't?" said the Colonel. "You're telling me you don't believe in things like ghosts or second sight?"

"Not in any of that," Parkins answered firmly.

"Well then," said the Colonel, "you must be some kind of Sadducee."

Parkins almost said that the Sadducees always seemed like the most reasonable people in the Bible, but he wasn't sure how much they were actually mentioned, so instead, he just laughed it off.

"Maybe I am," he said. "Here—pass me my club, please. Thanks. Sorry, Colonel, just one moment." He took his shot and then continued, "Now, about that wind whistling—let me explain my theory. People don't really understand how wind works. Fishermen and villagers especially have no tools like barometers, so they rely on guesses. If they see a strange person out on the beach whistling, and a strong wind shows up afterward, it's easy for them to think the person caused it. And maybe that person starts playing into it, enjoying the attention."

He paused and added, "Take last night, for example. I was actually whistling. I blew into a whistle twice, and the wind picked up almost right after. If anyone had seen me…"

The Colonel, who had been getting a little bored, perked up at that. "Whistling, were you? What kind of whistle was it? Take your shot first."

Afterward, Parkins answered, "About that whistle—it's a strange one. I think I left it in my room. I actually found it yesterday."

Then he explained how he had discovered it. The Colonel listened, grunted, and said that if it had been him, he wouldn't be using something that belonged to a bunch of Papists. He said you never knew what those people had been up to. From there, the Colonel started ranting about the local Vicar, who had announced last Sunday that there would be a church service on the Feast of St. Thomas. To the Colonel, that was a sure sign the Vicar was a secret Catholic—or maybe even a Jesuit.

Parkins didn't really follow the Colonel's logic, but he didn't argue. In fact, they got along so well that morning that neither of them mentioned going their separate ways after lunch.

They both kept playing decently in the afternoon—well enough that they didn't think about much else until it started getting dark. Only then did Parkins remember he'd meant to go back to the Templar ruins to do more digging. But he told himself it wasn't urgent. Any day would do. He might as well walk home with the Colonel.

As they turned a corner near the inn, a boy suddenly ran full-speed into the Colonel. Instead of running off, the boy grabbed onto him, panting and shaking. The Colonel's first reaction was to scold him, but he quickly realized the boy was terrified and couldn't even speak.

For a few minutes, they couldn't get a word out of him. When the boy finally caught his breath, he just started crying and still clung tightly to the Colonel's legs. It took some effort to pry him off—and even then, he kept wailing.

"What on earth is wrong with you? What happened? What did you see?" the two men asked.

"I saw it wave at me from the window!" the boy cried. "And I didn't like it!"

"Which window?" asked the Colonel, sounding annoyed. "Come on, pull yourself together, boy."

"It was the front window at the hotel," the boy said.

At this point, Parkins wanted to send the boy home, but the Colonel wouldn't allow it. He said it was dangerous to scare a child this badly, and if someone had been playing a prank, they needed to be held responsible. So, through several questions, they got the full story: the boy had been playing on the grass in front of the Globe Inn with some friends. After they left for tea, he was about to go too, when he looked up and saw something waving at him from the front window.

It looked like a figure dressed in white—he couldn't see the face—but it definitely didn't seem like a normal person. When asked if there was a light on in the room, he didn't know. He was also asked which window it was—top or bottom. He said it was the second one, the big window with two smaller ones on either side.

"All right, son," said the Colonel after a few more questions. "Head on home now. I expect it was just someone playing a trick. Next time, if something like that happens, be a brave boy—don't throw a rock or anything—but go tell the waiter or Mr. Simpson, the landlord, and say that I told you to."

The boy clearly didn't believe Mr. Simpson would listen to him, but the Colonel didn't notice and added, "And here's sixpence—no, wait, a shilling. Off you go now, and don't think about it anymore."

The boy ran off, nervously thanking them. Then the Colonel and Parkins walked to the front of the inn to check things out. There was only one window that matched the boy's description.

"Well, that's strange," said Parkins. "That's my room he was talking about. Do you want to come up and check? We should see if anyone's been in there."

They went upstairs, and Parkins reached for the door—then suddenly paused and checked his pockets.

"This is more serious than I thought," he said. "I remember locking this door before I left this morning. It's still locked—and here's the key." He held it up. "If the staff go into people's rooms while they're out, I really can't approve of that."

A bit flustered, he unlocked the door and lit the candles.

"Nothing looks out of place," he said.

"Except your bed," the Colonel pointed out.

"Oh, that's not my bed," Parkins replied. "I don't sleep in that one. But it does look like someone's been messing with it."

It really did—the covers were tangled and twisted like someone had been tossing and turning in it. Parkins thought for a moment.

"I must've messed it up last night while I was unpacking. Maybe someone came in later to make the bed, and the boy saw them through the window. Then they left and locked the door again. That must be it."

"Then ring the bell and ask," said the Colonel.

That seemed like a good idea to Parkins, so he rang. A maid came in and, after some back-and-forth, said she had made the bed in the morning while Parkins was still in the room. She hadn't been back since, and she didn't have a key—Mr. Simpson kept all the keys. He could say for sure if anyone else had been in the room.

This was confusing. Nothing had been stolen, and Parkins remembered his things well enough to know they hadn't been moved around. Mr. and Mrs. Simpson both insisted they hadn't given a key to anyone all day. Parkins, being fair, couldn't find anything suspicious in their behavior. He began to think the boy might have made the whole thing up to scare the Colonel.

The Colonel, though, was unusually quiet during dinner and afterward. As he said goodnight, he muttered in a low voice, "You know where to find me if you need anything tonight."

"Thank you, Colonel Wilson," Parkins replied. "I think I'll be fine. I don't expect to need anything. By the way," he added, "did I ever show you that old whistle I found? I don't think I did. Here it is."

The Colonel carefully examined it under the candlelight.

"Can you read the writing on it?" Parkins asked as he took it back.

"Not in this light. What are you planning to do with it?"

"Oh, well," Parkins said, "when I get back to Cambridge, I'll show it to some archaeologists there and see what they think. If they say it's important, I might donate it to a museum."

"Hmm," grunted the Colonel. "You might be right. But if it were mine, I'd toss it straight into the sea. No point in saying more—I know you won't listen. But maybe you'll learn from this. I hope so. Good night."

He turned and walked away, leaving Parkins at the bottom of the stairs. Soon, they were both in their rooms.

By bad luck, there were no curtains or blinds on the windows in Parkins's room. He hadn't minded the night before, but now the bright moonlight was shining straight onto his bed, and he knew it would probably wake him later. Annoyed, he came up with a clever solution. Using a travel blanket, some safety pins, a stick, and an umbrella, he built a screen to block the moonlight. Once that was done, he got into bed and began reading a heavy book until he felt sleepy. Then he looked around the room, blew out the candle, and lay down to sleep.

He must have slept for about an hour when a sudden crash woke him up. His makeshift screen had fallen apart, and now the moonlight was shining right in his face. It was frustrating. Should he get up and fix it, or try to sleep as it was?

As he lay there thinking, he suddenly turned over and opened his eyes. He was sure he'd just heard a noise coming from the empty bed on the other side of the room. Maybe there were rats? Tomorrow he'd ask for the bed to be removed. But now it was quiet again. Then he heard the sound again—soft rustling and shaking. It was too much noise for just a rat.

I can only imagine how confused and scared he felt—like in one of those vivid, unsettling dreams. Because then, he saw something truly terrifying: someone—or something—sat up in the empty bed.

Parkins jumped out of his own bed in a panic and ran to the window where he'd left a stick, the only thing he had to defend himself. But that turned out to be a mistake. The figure in the bed moved with a smooth, unnatural motion and stood up between the two beds, right in front of the door. Parkins froze. The idea of trying to run past it horrified him. He didn't know why, but he couldn't bear to touch it—or to be touched by it. He would've rather jumped out the window than let that happen.

The figure stood in a dark shadow, so he couldn't see its face. Then it began to move, hunched over, arms out like it was feeling around blindly. That's when Parkins realized it must be unable to see—it seemed to grope and search as if it were lost.

It turned partway toward the bed Parkins had just left and quickly moved to it, bending over and running its hands across the pillows. Watching this made Parkins shudder with disgust and fear. The thing seemed to realize no one was in the bed and stepped into the moonlight, turning toward the window.

That's when Parkins saw its face—and it's not something he likes to talk about. Once, though, I heard him describe it: a horrible face, like a twisted mess of linen. He wouldn't say what kind of expression it had, but whatever he saw on it nearly drove him mad.

He didn't have time to keep looking. The creature suddenly moved to the center of the room, searching with its arms. One edge of its clothing brushed against Parkins's face, and he couldn't stop himself from crying out in disgust. That was all it needed. The thing instantly turned and jumped toward him.

Parkins backed through the window, screaming loudly. The creature's face came right up to his. And then—just in time—help arrived.

The Colonel burst through the door and saw the awful scene by the window. When he reached them, only Parkins was still there. He collapsed into the room, unconscious, while the other bed was now just a mess of tangled sheets on the floor.

The Colonel didn't ask questions. He kept others away and helped Parkins back to bed. Then he wrapped himself in a blanket and stayed in the room the rest of the night.

The next morning, Rogers showed up—more welcome now than he would've been the day before. The three men had a long private talk in Parkins's room. When it was over, the Colonel left the inn holding a small object between his fingers. He walked to the shore and threw it as far into the sea as he could. Later that day, smoke rose from behind the Globe Inn.

I don't remember exactly what explanation was given to the hotel staff or guests, but somehow they cleared Parkins of any suspicion of being drunk or mad, and the inn kept its good reputation.

It's pretty clear what would've happened to Parkins if the Colonel hadn't arrived when he did. He either would've jumped out the window or lost his mind. Still, it's not clear what more that thing could've done besides scare him. It didn't seem to have any real body—only bedclothes that formed its shape. The Colonel, who remembered something similar happening in India, believed the creature couldn't actually harm anyone unless they gave in to fear. Its real power was how terrifying it looked. The whole thing, he said, only made him more certain about his negative opinion of the Catholic Church.

There's not much else to tell. As you might guess, Parkins's views on certain subjects aren't as firm as they used to be. His nerves haven't fully recovered either. Even now, just seeing a white robe hanging behind a door can shake him up, and spotting a scarecrow late in the afternoon has left him lying awake more than once.

The Treasure of Abbot Thomas

I

Even today, the monks at Steinfeld Abbey often talk about a hidden treasure left behind by Abbot Thomas. They've searched for it many times but never found it. According to legend, Thomas buried a huge amount of gold somewhere around the monastery while he was still young and healthy. When people asked him where it was, he would just laugh and say, "Job, John, and Zechariah will tell you—or your descendants." Sometimes he added that he wouldn't mind if someone found it.

One of the abbot's most important projects was adding a large stained-glass window to the east end of the church's south aisle. It showed beautifully painted images, and his portrait and family crest were included in the design. He also restored almost the entire abbot's house, dug a well in its courtyard, and decorated it with carved marble. He died suddenly at the age of 72, in the year 1529.

The person studying this story was an antiquarian—someone interested in old things—and he was trying to track down what had happened to the stained-glass windows from Steinfeld Abbey. After many monasteries in Germany and Belgium were closed during the Revolution, lots of their stained glass was brought to England. Today, you can find it in churches, cathedrals, and private chapels across the country. Steinfeld Abbey was one of the main sources of this glass, and much of it can still be identified either by inscriptions or the scenes they depict.

The passage about Abbot Thomas had caught the antiquarian's attention because it helped him solve a mystery. In a private chapel—he didn't say exactly where—he had seen three large stained-glass figures, each taking up its own window panel. They were clearly made by the same artist, probably a German from the 1500s, but the antiquarian hadn't been able to figure out exactly where they came from.

The figures were of Job the Patriarch, John the Evangelist, and Zechariah the Prophet. Each one held a scroll or book with a quote. But the quotes weren't quite like any he'd seen before in the usual Latin Bible. For example, Job's scroll read, "There is a place for gold where it is hidden," though the real verse says something a little different. John's scroll said, "They have on their clothing a writing which no one knows," which mixes lines from different verses. Zechariah's quote, though, was accurate: "Upon one stone are seven eyes."

This strange grouping had puzzled the antiquarian. There was no clear reason why these three people would be shown together. He guessed they might have been part of a bigger group of prophets and apostles that once filled the upper windows of a large church.

But the passage from the old book gave him a new clue. It said that Abbot Thomas used to mention these three names—Job, John, and Zechariah—whenever he was asked about his treasure. And since Thomas had also paid for a window at Steinfeld Abbey around 1520, it now seemed likely that these three figures had been part of that very window. Maybe they were the abbot's way of giving a clue about the treasure's hiding place.

Excited by this idea, the antiquarian decided to revisit the chapel and examine the glass more closely. What he found confirmed his theory. The style and craftsmanship matched the right time and place.

In another window, made from glass bought at the same time, he even found the crest of Abbot Thomas von Eschenhausen.

As he continued his study, the idea of the hidden treasure kept coming back to him. The strange quotes on the scrolls might have been hints. The first one, especially, seemed to suggest something buried. So, he carefully took notes on every detail of the window that might help solve the mystery. Then, back at his house in Berkshire, he spent many long nights reviewing his drawings and ideas.

After a few weeks, he told his servant to pack their things. They were heading on a short trip abroad—but where they were going, he didn't yet say.

II

Mr. Gregory, the Rector of Parsbury, stepped outside early one crisp autumn morning before breakfast. The air was cool and fresh, and he wanted to enjoy it while waiting for the postman. His children came with him, full of energy and asking him all sorts of random questions, just for fun. Before he could answer more than a few, the postman arrived.

Among the letters was one with a foreign stamp. The kids immediately began arguing over who would get to keep it. The handwriting was rough, but clearly English. When Mr. Gregory opened it and looked at the signature, he realized it was from William Brown, the loyal valet of his friend, Mr. Somerton. The letter read:

HONOURED SIR,

I'm very worried about Master, and I'm writing this at his request. He's had a terrible shock and hasn't gotten out of bed since. I've never seen him like this before, so it makes sense he wants you, sir. He says to let you know the quickest way here is to go to Coblenz and then take a carriage. I hope this all makes sense. I haven't been sleeping and I'm quite upset.

If I may be bold, sir, it would truly be a relief to see a familiar British face in the middle of all these foreigners.

Your faithful servant,

William Brown

P.S. The village is called Steinfeld.

You can probably imagine the shock and rush that followed in Mr. Gregory's quiet home after reading that letter. That very same day, he boarded a train to London, got on a boat to Antwerp, and took another train to Coblenz. From there, reaching the village of Steinfeld wasn't hard.

Now, I have to admit I've never visited Steinfeld myself. The two people who did—Mr. Gregory and Mr. Somerton—could only give a vague and gloomy idea of what it looked like. From what I understand, it's a small village with a large church that's been stripped of its old decorations. Around the church are several large, crumbling buildings, mostly from the 1600s, when the abbey was rebuilt in a grand and fancy style like many others across Europe. I've never had the urge to visit, even though it might be more interesting than they described—aside from one particular thing I wouldn't want to see.

Mr. Somerton and his valet had been staying at the only decent inn in the village. When Mr. Gregory arrived, his driver took him straight there. Mr. Brown was waiting at the door. Usually calm and professional back home in Berkshire, he now looked completely out of place in a light-colored suit, clearly anxious and uncomfortable. When he saw Mr. Gregory's familiar face, he was overwhelmed with relief but could barely get out more than:

"I'm so glad to see you, sir. I know Master will be too."

"How is he, Brown?" Mr. Gregory asked right away.

"I think he's a little better now, sir, thank you—but he's been through something terrible. I think he might be asleep right now."

"What happened, exactly? Your letter didn't explain much. Was it an accident?"

"Well, sir, I'm not sure if I should say. Master really wanted to tell you himself. But I can say this—he's not hurt physically. No broken bones, thank goodness."

"What did the doctor say?" Mr. Gregory asked.

By then they had reached Mr. Somerton's bedroom door and were speaking in hushed voices. Mr. Gregory stepped forward and reached for the doorknob, his fingers brushing over the wooden panels. Before Brown could reply, a sudden scream burst from inside the room.

"For God's sake, who's out there?" a voice cried. "Brown, is that you?"

"Yes, sir—it's me, sir, and Mr. Gregory," Brown quickly replied. From inside the room came a deep sigh of relief.

They stepped in. The room was dim, shaded from the afternoon sunlight. Mr. Gregory felt a wave of pity when he saw his friend sitting up in bed, his face pale and sweaty with fear—so unlike his usual calm self. Still, he stretched out a trembling hand to greet him.

"Better now that you're here, my dear Gregory," Mr. Somerton said in response to the Rector's first question—and it was clearly true.

After just a few minutes of conversation, Mr. Somerton seemed much more like himself again. Brown later said he hadn't seen his master this stable in days. Mr. Somerton even managed to eat a decent meal and confidently said he thought he'd be ready to travel to Coblenz within a day.

"But there's one thing," he said, suddenly looking anxious again—something that worried Mr. Gregory. "Something I need you to do for me, Gregory. Please," he added, placing a hand on Gregory's to stop any questions, "don't ask me what it is or why I need it done. I'm not ready to explain. Talking about it would set me back again—it would undo all the good you've done by coming here."

"The only thing I will say is this: you won't be in any danger at all. Brown knows what to do and will show you in the morning. It's just a matter of putting something back... of keeping it where it belongs. No, I still can't talk about it. Can you call Brown?"

"All right, Somerton," said Mr. Gregory, walking to the door. "I won't press for answers. And if it's really as simple as you say, I'll be happy to take care of it first thing in the morning."

"I knew I could count on you, Gregory. Thank you—truly. I owe you more than I can say. Now, here comes Brown. Brown, a word."

"Shall I go?" asked Mr. Gregory.

"No, no—stay right there," said Somerton. "Brown, in the morning—first thing—you'll take the Rector to... you know where." (Brown nodded, looking serious and uneasy.) "You and he will put it back. There's nothing to be afraid of, not in daylight. You know what I'm talking about—it's on the step, right where we left it." (Brown swallowed hard and nodded again, still unable to speak.)

"And one more thing, Gregory. If you can avoid asking Brown questions about this, I'd really appreciate it. If everything goes well, I believe I'll be able to tell you the whole story by tomorrow evening—start to finish. For now, I'll say good night. Brown's staying with me tonight. If I were you, I'd lock your door. Really—do lock it. People around here expect it, and it's for the best. Good night."

They said their goodbyes. Later that night, Mr. Gregory thought he heard soft noises around his door, as if someone—or something—was fumbling at the bottom of it. He woke up a few times and listened. Whether it was just his imagination, brought on by being in a strange place in the middle of something mysterious, he never knew. But for the rest of his life, he believed he'd heard those sounds—two or three times, between midnight and morning.

He got up with the sun and went out with Brown not long after. Whatever Mr. Somerton had asked him to do, it was confusing, but not hard or frightening. Within thirty minutes of leaving the inn, it was done. I won't reveal just yet what that task was.

Later that morning, Mr. Somerton—looking much stronger—was able to leave Steinfeld. That evening, whether they were in Coblenz or somewhere else along the way, he finally sat down to explain everything, just as he'd promised. Brown was there too, but no one ever found out how much he really understood. He never said, and I don't know either.

III

This is what Mr. Somerton shared:

"You both already know that the reason for my trip was to investigate something connected to some old stained glass windows in Lord D——'s private chapel. Everything really started with this passage from an old book, which I'd like you to look at."

At this point, Mr. Somerton went over the background again, which we've already heard.

"On my second visit to the chapel," he continued, "I planned to take detailed notes on everything—the figures, the writing, even small scratches or marks that might have seemed accidental. I started with the scrolls that had writing on them. The first one, the one held by Job, said, 'There is a place for the gold where it is hidden.' That line was clearly changed on purpose, and I believed it had to be a clue about the treasure. So I focused on the next line, the one held by St. John: 'They have on their vestures a writing which no man knoweth.'

"You're probably wondering the same thing I did—was there actually any writing on the robes of the figures? I couldn't see any. Each of the three figures had a thick black border on their cloaks, which stood out and honestly looked a bit ugly. I was stuck, and I have to admit, I might have given up right then, just like the Canons of Steinfeld had, if I hadn't gotten lucky.

"There was quite a bit of dust on the glass, and while I was working, Lord D—— walked in. He noticed how dirty my hands were and kindly offered to have the window cleaned. He sent for a Turk's head broom, the kind used for dusting, and the man started brushing the glass. Apparently, the broom had a rough bit on it, because when it passed over the black border on one of the cloaks, I noticed a long scratch—and right away, I saw a yellow stain underneath. I stopped the cleaner and quickly climbed the ladder to look closer. Sure enough, there was a yellow stain, and it looked like a thick black paint had been brushed on top of the glass long after it was made. That paint could be scraped off easily without damaging the glass underneath.

"So I carefully scraped a little away, and I could hardly believe what I saw. Actually, I'm sure you've already guessed—underneath the black paint were a few large yellow letters on clear glass. You can imagine how thrilled I was.

"I told Lord D—— that I had found what looked like an old inscription, possibly very important, and asked for his permission to uncover the rest. He didn't hesitate at all and told me to go ahead. Then, thankfully, he had to leave for an appointment, which gave me some space to work.

"I got to it right away. The black paint came off easily—it had broken down with time—and in less than two hours, I had cleared the black borders on all three windows. Just like the scroll had said, each of the figures had hidden writing on their cloaks that no one had seen before."

"This discovery proved to me, without a doubt, that I was on the right path. Now, let me tell you what the hidden message actually said. While I was cleaning the glass, I made a point not to read the writing right away. I wanted to save the surprise until I had revealed the entire inscription. But once I had finished and read it—my dear Gregory, I was so disappointed I could have cried. It just looked like a mess of random letters, like someone had shaken them up in a hat. Here's what I found:

Job:

DREVICIOPEDMOOMSMVIVLISLCAVIBASBATAOVT

St John:

RDIIEAMRLESIPVSPODSEEIRSETTAAESGIAVNNR

Zechariah:

DREVICIOPEDMOOMSMVIVLISLCAVIBASBATAOVT

"At first, I felt totally stuck. But then I realized that it had to be a code—a cipher of some kind. And I figured it was probably a simple one, since it came from so long ago. So I carefully copied down the letters.

"While doing that, I noticed something else that convinced me I was right. After I finished writing down the letters on Job's robe, I counted them. There were thirty-eight. And right then, I spotted a small scratch on the glass that read 'xxxviii'—which is 38 in Roman numerals. I found similar markings on the other two windows. That told me the glassmaker had been given very specific instructions by Abbot Thomas and took care to get the letters just right.

"After that, I examined every inch of the glass, looking for more clues. I didn't forget the verse on Zechariah's scroll—'Upon one stone are seven eyes'—but I figured that referred to some actual stone near the hidden treasure, something that could only be found on site.

"I took all the notes, sketches, and tracings I could, and then went back to Parsbury to try and break the code. It was torture! At first, I thought I was clever. I tried looking for the key in some old books on secret writing—Trithemius's Steganographia, Selenius's Cryptographia, Bacon's De Augmentis Scientiarum, and others. But I found nothing that helped. Then I tried using the 'most common letter' method, starting with Latin and then German. That didn't work either.

"So I returned to my notes, hoping maybe Abbot Thomas had left a clue in the window itself. I looked at the colors and patterns on the robes—nothing. No helpful background scenes. The only thing left to study was the way the figures were posed.

"My notes said:

Job—scroll in left hand, one finger on right hand pointing up.

John—book in left hand, giving a blessing with two fingers on the right hand.

Zechariah—scroll in left hand, three fingers on right hand pointing up.

"That's when it hit me: maybe the number of fingers meant something. One, two, three... could it be the key?

"My dear Gregory," said Mr. Somerton, resting a hand on his friend's knee, "that was the key. It didn't work right away, but after a few tries, I got it. After the first letter, skip one; after the next, skip two; after that, skip three—and so on. Look at what I found. I've underlined the letters that formed words:

[D]R[E]VI[C]IOP[E]D[M]OO[M]SMV[I]V[L]IS[L]CAV[I]B[A]S B[A]TAO[V]T

[R]DI[I]EAM[R]L[E]SI[P]VSP[O]D[S]EE[I]RSE[T]T[A]AE[S]GI A[V]N[N]R

F[T]EEA[I]L[N]QD[P]VAI[V]M[T]LE[E]ATT[O]H[I]OO[N]V MC[A]A[T].H.Q.E.

"You can see the message beginning to appear:

'Decem millia auri reposita sunt in puteo in at...'

That means: 'Ten thousand pieces of gold are laid up in a well in...' followed by a word starting with at.

"I tried the same trick on the leftover letters, but it didn't work again. That's when I noticed the three dots at the end. Maybe they meant the rest of the message had to be read differently.

"Then I remembered the book Sertum Steinfeldense mentioned that Abbot Thomas had built a well in the courtyard—puteus in atrio. That must be the missing word: atrio (in the courtyard).

"So I wrote down all the letters I hadn't used yet. That gave me this:

RVIIOPDOOSMVVISCAVBSBTAOTDIEAMLSIVSPDEERS
ETAEGIANRFEEALQDVAIMLEATTHOOVMCA.H.Q.E.

"I knew the next letters I needed were r, i, o to finish atrio, and those showed up near the beginning. I noticed that every other letter seemed to spell something. When I tried that, here's what I got:

'rio domus abbatialis de Steinfeld a me, Thoma, qui posui custodem super ea. Gare à qui la touche.'

"It means:

'in the courtyard of the Abbot's house of Steinfeld by me, Thomas, who have set a guardian over it. Beware to whoever touches it.'

"Those last words—Gare à qui la touche—are a motto that Abbot Thomas used. I'd seen it along with his family crest on another piece of stained glass at Lord D——'s place. He slipped that warning into his secret message, even though the grammar doesn't quite fit."

"Well, Gregory, what would anyone have done in my place? Honestly, could anyone resist going straight to Steinfeld to follow the trail all the way to the source? I know I couldn't. As soon as I could make the travel arrangements, I was on my way, and soon I was staying at the inn you saw for yourself.

"I have to admit, I felt a mix of emotions—on one hand, I worried I'd be disappointed, and on the other, I was afraid. What if the well Abbot Thomas mentioned had been destroyed? Or worse, what if someone had already found the treasure by accident? And then"—his voice shook a little—"I couldn't stop thinking about what the Abbot said about a guardian watching over the treasure. I'll say more about that later, but for now, I'll leave it at that.

"Brown and I began searching the area right away. I told people I was just interested in the old ruins, so we made a stop at the church, even though I was itching to look elsewhere. Still, it was worth seeing. I looked at the windows, especially the one at the east end of the south aisle. There were still a few fragments left—Abbot Thomas's coat of arms was there, and a small figure holding a scroll that read 'They have eyes, and shall not see'. That felt like a sarcastic message from the Abbot to the Canons.

"But the main goal, of course, was finding the Abbot's house. There isn't a fixed spot for it in a monastery's layout like there is for the chapter-house or the dormitory. I didn't want to ask too many questions in case it reminded anyone about the treasure, so I searched on my own. Luckily, it didn't take long. That U-shaped courtyard southeast of the church, the one surrounded by old, unused buildings and grass-covered stones—that was it. I was thrilled to see it hadn't been repurposed and that it was close to our inn, not overlooked by any nearby homes. Only orchards and fields lay beyond. The stone really glowed in that soft, yellow sunset we had on Tuesday evening.

"Now, what about the well? You saw it yourself—it's quite remarkable. The edge is probably Italian marble, and the carvings looked Italian too. They showed scenes like Eliezer meeting Rebekah, and Jacob opening the well for Rachel. Nothing suspicious—Abbot Thomas must have left out any of his usual snarky messages on purpose to avoid drawing attention.

"I looked over the whole thing closely. It was a square stone well with an open side, and a stone arch above, with a wheel for the rope—still in working condition. It had clearly been used within the last 60 years, maybe even more recently. As for how deep it was, I'd guess about 60 or 70 feet. What really caught my attention was how easy the

Abbot seemed to make it to get inside. As you saw, large stone blocks were built into the wall, forming a kind of spiral staircase going down inside the well.

"It almost seemed too perfect. I worried it might be a trick—maybe the steps would collapse under my weight. But I tested several with both my body and my walking stick, and they were solid. So, I decided that Brown and I would go down there that very night.

"I had come prepared. I brought strong rope, harness straps, crossbars to grip, lanterns, candles, and crowbars. Everything fit neatly in a carpet bag, so no one would think anything of it. I checked that the rope was long enough and that the wheel still worked, and then we went back to the inn for dinner.

"I carefully brought it up with the innkeeper and hinted that I might go for a walk with my servant around nine that evening—just to make a sketch of the ruins by moonlight. (Heaven forgive the lie!) I didn't mention the well, and I don't think I ever will. Honestly"—he shivered—"I think I already know more about that place than anyone else in Steinfeld. And to tell you the truth, I don't want to know any more."

"Now we get to the most important part of the story. I hate remembering it, Gregory, but I think it's best that I tell it exactly as it happened. Brown and I left the inn around nine o'clock with our bag, and we didn't draw any attention. We slipped out through the back of the yard and followed a small alley that took us to the edge of the village. In just five minutes, we were at the well.

"We sat on the edge for a little while, just to make sure no one was nearby or watching us. The only sounds were from some horses quietly grazing somewhere farther down the hill. The moon was full and bright, so we had plenty of light to set up the rope properly over the wheel. I fastened a harness around my chest and under my arms. We tied the rope tightly to a metal ring in the stone. Brown held the lantern and followed behind me while I took the crowbar, and we started going down the steps carefully, testing each one before stepping on it. We kept looking at the walls, hoping to spot some kind of special marking.

"I counted the steps quietly as we went. By the time we reached the thirty-eighth, I hadn't seen anything unusual. Even at that step, there wasn't a visible mark. I started to feel discouraged. Could it be that the Abbot's message had just been a trick?

"Then, at the forty-ninth step, the staircase ended. I felt my heart sink. I began to climb back up, and when I got back to the thirty-eighth step—with Brown and the lantern just above me—I studied the wall where I'd seen something slightly odd. There wasn't a clear mark, but the surface looked a little smoother, maybe even like it was made of cement, not stone.

"I hit it hard with the crowbar. It made a hollow sound—though I thought that could just be because we were in a well. But then a large chunk of the cement broke off and fell at my feet, and underneath, I saw something carved into the stone. I had found the Abbot's hiding place! I still feel a bit proud just thinking about it.

"A few more taps, and the rest of the cement came off. Behind it was a flat stone about two feet across, and it had a cross carved into it. At first, I was disappointed again. But then you, Brown, said something I'll never forget—you said, 'That's a funny-looking cross. Looks like a bunch of eyes.'

"I grabbed the lantern and looked closer. You were right. The cross was made of seven carved eyes—four going up and down, and three across. That was it! That explained the last line from the window: the 'stone with seven eyes.' Everything the Abbot had said so far had been right. But now, the warning about the 'guardian' came back into my mind and made me nervous again. Still, I couldn't stop now.

"I didn't let myself hesitate. I cleared the cement all around the stone and used the crowbar to pry it up on the right side. It moved easily—it was a light slab I could lift myself. Underneath was a hollow space. I lifted the stone out carefully and placed it beside me. I had a feeling it might be important to put it back later.

"I paused for several minutes, sitting on the step just above. I can't really explain why. Maybe I wanted to see if anything awful would come out. But nothing did. I lit a candle and slowly lowered it into the hole to check for bad air and to see what was inside. The flame flickered a bit, like the air was stale, but after a moment, it steadied.

"The space went back a little and stretched to the left and right. I could just make out some pale, rounded shapes that might've been bags. I knew there was no point in waiting any longer. I turned to face the opening, leaned in, and slowly reached my arm inside to feel along the right side…"

"Just get me a glass of brandy, Brown. I'll keep going in a minute, Gregory…

"So, I reached my hand to the right and touched something curved—it felt sort of like leather. It was damp and clearly part of something heavy and full. There was nothing scary about it at first. I got braver, and using both hands, I pulled it closer. It was heavier than I expected but moved easily enough. As I was pulling it out, my left elbow accidentally knocked over the candle and put it out.

"I had just pulled the thing to the opening when Brown suddenly shouted and ran up the steps with the lantern. He'll tell you why in a minute. I was startled and looked after him. I saw him pause at the top, then walk a little farther away. A moment later he called back softly, 'All right, sir,' so I kept pulling out the large bag, now in complete darkness.

"It rested on the edge for a moment, then slipped forward onto my chest—and wrapped its arms around my neck.

"Gregory, I'm telling you exactly what happened. I now know the worst kind of terror a man can feel without going insane. I can barely explain it, but I'll try. I smelled the awful stench of mold. I felt a cold, clammy face pressing against mine, sliding over it slowly. I don't know how many limbs it had—arms, legs, tentacles—but they clung to me. Brown says I screamed like an animal and fell backward off the step. The creature must have slipped down with me.

"Thankfully, the safety strap around me held. Brown didn't panic and somehow had the strength to pull me all the way back up and over the edge of the well. How he managed it, I don't know, and I doubt he does either. I think he hid our tools in one of the nearby abandoned buildings, and after a great struggle, he got me back to the inn. I couldn't explain anything, and Brown doesn't speak German. The next morning, I told the people at the inn I'd had a bad fall in the abbey ruins—which I guess they believed.

"Before I go on, I want you to hear what Brown saw while this was happening. Brown, tell the Rector what you told me."

Brown spoke quietly, nervously: "Well, sir, this is what happened. Master was down by the hole, and I was holding the lantern, just watching. Then I heard something splash in the water from above, I thought. I looked up and saw a head staring down at us. I must've said something and raised the lantern—and that's when I saw the face. It was awful, sir. An old man's face, sunken in, and smiling—like he was laughing. I rushed up the steps quick as anything, but when I got there, no one was around. There hadn't been time for anyone, especially not an old man, to get away. I checked around the well, but nothing. Then I heard master scream, and when I looked back, he was hanging by the rope—and like he says, I don't know how I managed to pull him up."

"You hear that, Gregory?" Somerton said. "Do you have any explanation for what he saw?"

"It's all so horrifying and unreal," Gregory replied, "but I did think that maybe—just maybe—the person who set the trap came to watch it succeed."

"Yes, Gregory, exactly. I can't think of a better explanation. I think it was the Abbot himself...

"Well, there's not much left to say. I had a terrible night. Brown stayed with me. The next day, I couldn't even get out of bed. There was no doctor nearby, and even if there had been, I doubt he could have helped. I had Brown write to you, and I spent another horrible night waiting for you.

"And Gregory, I'm certain—absolutely certain—that something was outside my door that whole second night. Maybe more than one thing. It wasn't just the soft noises I kept hearing. It was the smell—that same awful moldy smell. I had Brown burn every piece of clothing I wore that first night, but the smell still filled the room. Worse, it came from under the door. But as soon as the first light of dawn came through, it disappeared—so did the noises. That convinced me the thing, or things, could only move in the dark. I was sure they'd stay powerless if someone just sealed the hole again. But I couldn't send Brown to do it alone, and I definitely couldn't tell anyone local.

"So that's my story. If you don't believe it, I can't help that. But I think you do."

"I do," said Gregory. "I don't see any other explanation. I saw the well myself, and I think I even saw the bags inside. And to be honest, Somerton, I think something was watching my door last night too."

"I'm not surprised, Gregory. But thankfully, it's all over now. Did anything happen while you were there today?"

"Not much," Gregory answered. "Brown and I got the stone back into place easily. He fixed it tight with the wedges and tools you told him to bring. We covered it with mud so it blends in with the rest of the wall. But I did notice one carving on the well that I don't think you saw. It was a disturbing, ugly figure—kind of like a toad—and there was a label underneath it with the words: 'Depositum custodi.'"

"Which means," Somerton added quietly, "'Keep that which is committed to you.'"

Thank You for Reading

Dear Reader,

We hope this timeless classic has sparked your imagination and enriched your literary journey. Now that you've turned the final page, we want to share a vision for the future of reading—one where every classic you've ever wanted to explore is at your fingertips, in a format that best suits your life.

We'd like to invite you to gain immediate, unlimited digital & audiobook access to hundreds of the most treasured literary classics ever written—along with the option to secure deluxe paperback, hardcover & box set editions at printing cost. Together, we can spark a new global literary renaissance alongside our small, independent publishing house called "The Library of Alexandria."

Thousands of years ago, the Library of Alexandria stood as a beacon of knowledge—until it was lost to history. We aim to reignite that spirit of preservation and discovery right now, in the modern age—only this time, it's accessible to all, in every language and every format.

Picture a world where every timeless classic, novel, poem, or philosophical treatise is not only available to read but also updated for today's readers—modernized, translated into any language or dialect, and ready to enjoy in any format you choose, whether that is in an eBook, audiobook, paperback, or deluxe hardcover & box set version a printing cost.

By joining our movement to rebuild the modern Library of Alexandria, you become part of an unprecedented mission to offer:

- **Unlimited Audiobook & eBook Access to the Greatest Classics of All Time**

  Instantly explore thousands of legendary works, from Plato and Shakespeare to Jane Austen and Leo Tolstoy. All are instantly ready to read or listen to, giving you a complete literary universe at your fingertips.

- **Paperback & Deluxe Editions at Printing Costs:**

  Purchase any title in a paperback, deluxe hardbound, or deluxe boxset edition at printing costs, shipped right to your doorstep. Curate your personal library of Alexandria with editions worthy of display—crafted to last, designed to captivate, and delivered straight to your door.

- **Modern translations for Contemporary Readers in all languages and dialects**

  Discover a vast selection of classics reimagined in clear, current language—no more struggling with outdated phrases or obscure references. Next to the original versions, we aim to offer translations in as many languages and dialects as possible.

  As we continue our translation efforts and add new languages, readers everywhere can connect with these works as if they were written today. By bridging linguistic divides, you're contributing to ensuring that these timeless stories become more meaningful, accessible, and inspiring for people across the globe.

- **Your Personal Library of Alexandria:**

  Over the months and years, you'll curate a unique physical archive of classics—each volume a testament to your taste, curiosity, and love of knowledge. It's not just about owning books—it's about curating a cultural legacy you'll cherish and pass down for generations to come.

- **Join a Global Literary Renaissance:**

Your support fuels an ongoing mission: allowing us to reinvest in offering deluxe print editions (including special boxsets) at their true cost, broaden the range of available formats and translations, and extend the reach of these works to new audiences worldwide. By joining today, you're not just preserving a legacy of masterpieces; you set in motion a powerful wave of literary accessibility.

We are more than a publisher—we're a movement, and we can't do it alone. Your support lets us scale our mission, preserving and reimagining history's greatest works for tomorrow's readers.

Become a Torchbearer of knowledge.

Thank you for picking up this book and allowing us into your literary journey. As you turn the pages, know that you're part of something larger: a global effort to keep these stories alive, share their wisdom across borders and generations, and spark a true cultural revival for the modern era.

If this resonates with you—please consider taking the next step by visiting:

www.libraryofalexandria.com

With gratitude and a shared love of knowledge,

The Modern Library of Alexandria Team

Visit:

www.libraryofalexandria.com

Or scan the code below:

www.ingramcontent.com/pod-product-compliance
Lightning Source LLC
Chambersburg PA
CBHW012205030726
47494CB00022B/2351